THREE TALES OF
LOVE AND DEATH

Middle East Literature in Translation
Michael Beard and Adnan Haydar
Series Editors

"The things which have been made are eternity and
the things which shall be made are everlastingness
and that eternity is the day and everlastingness the night."

From the papyrus of Ani, The Transformation of Osiris,
Egyptian Book of the Dead. Artwork by Michelle Slater.
Courtesy of the artist.

THREE TALES OF
LOVE AND DEATH

OUT EL KOULOUB

Translated and with an Introduction by
NAYRA ATIYA

SYRACUSE UNIVERSITY PRESS

Trois contes de l'amour et de la mort was originally published in French in 1940 by Editions Correa, Paris.

The paper used in this publication meets the minimum requirements of American National Standard for Information Sciences—Permanence of Paper for Printed Library Materials, ANSI Z39.48-1984.

Library of Congress Cataloging-in-Publication Data

Out el Kouloub.
    [Trois contes de l'amour et de la mort. English]
    Three tales of love and death / Out el Kouloub ; translated with an introduction by Nayra Atiya.
       p. cm. — (Middle East literature in translation)
       ISBN 0-8156-0627-3 (cloth : alk. paper)
       I. Title: 3 tales of love and death. II. Atiya, Nayra. III. Title. IV. Series.

PQ3989.2.O86 T7613 2000
843'.912—dc21   99-086342

Manufactured in the United States of America

This translation is dedicated to
Henriette Sakakini, Janet Lippman Abu Lughod,
and Jill Reintjes.

OUT EL KOULOUB (1899–1968) was an Egyptian author who wrote in French. A member of the Muslim aristocracy, she fled Cairo in the early 1960s after Nasser came to power.

NAYRA ATIYA was born in Egypt, was educated in the United States, and now lives in New York City. Her oral histories of five Egyptian women, *Khul-Khaal* (Syracuse University Press), won the 1990 UNICEF Prize for the best book on women, children, and development. Atiya's translations of other novels by Out el Kouloub, *Ramza* and *Zanouba,* are also published by Syracuse University Press.

CONTENTS

Translator's Acknowledgments   ix

Translator's Introduction   xi

Zariffa and Ahmad

Prologue   3

1. A Bedouin Family   3
2. Ahmad Abdou   5
3. Mouled of El Sayyed Badawi   7
4. Idyll in the Fields   11
5. Mabrouk el Gabali   14
6. Engagement   16
7. Tears and Kisses   19
8. The War   20
9. A Father's Cruelty   23
10. The Wedding   26
11. The Returned   30
12. The Burial   31
13. The Lovers   34

Nazira

1. Marriage   39
2. The Young Spouse   43

3. The Perfume Merchant   46

4. The *Codia*   50

5. The Jeweler   53

6. The *Zar*   58

7. Love Time   62

8. Passion and Forgetfulness   67

9. Tragedy   72

10. The Nile   80

Zaheira

1. Mazghouna   87

2. Elhamy   90

3. Spring   95

4. A Master   98

5. Gazbiyya   102

6. Freedom   105

7. Love   108

8. Mounira   111

9. Dreams   115

10. A Modern Wedding   119

11. Sheikh Gaafar's Third Wife   122

12. Seashells   126

13. Servant and Concubine   130

TRANSLATOR'S ACKNOWLEDGMENTS

I would like to extend special thanks to Asma el Bakri for first suggesting I translate the work of Out el Kouloub; to Father Qanawati of the Dominican Institute, Cairo, for the only copy I was ever able to find of *Trois contes de l'amour et de la mort;* to Robert Alford for his steady and invaluable editorial help; to Mary Frank for being—even from afar—an inspiration on the creative path; to Janet Lippman Abu Lughod for her sturdy support and example; to Melissa Solomon for cheering me on; to Mary Megalli in Taos, New Mexico, and Andrea Rugh in Woods Hole, Massachusetts, for hosting me as I worked; to Ragai Makar for his help and encouragement; to Donette Atiyah, Deena Abu Lughod, and Michelle Slater for their insightful comments; to Gary and Karlan Sick for their cheerful support always; to Margaret Kornfeld for helping me maintain an even keel; to Cynthia Maude-Gembler, a sterling editor; to Katrina Atiya Malkin and Adam Atiya Walker for championing their mother's work and then some; and to my mother, Lola Atiya, for her unwavering support.

Special thanks also to three spiritual communities that have, for years, provided me with support and inspiration along the way: Jivamukti Yoga Center, New York City, and especially my cherished teachers Sharon Gannon and David Life; Also Krishna Das Kagel, Shyam Das, and Ram Das; Ananda Ashram, Monroe, New York, and the inimitable Joan Suval; and Calvary Baptist Church, Salt Lake City, Utah, whose bright-burning pastor, Doctor France A. Davis, is an example of loving, energetic leadership.

Finally, thanks to Mary Selden Evans, my new editor, for her enthusiastic response to my translation of these stories and for her efforts in bringing this book to the finish line, and to the excellent team at Syracuse University Press.

TRANSLATOR'S INTRODUCTION

In 1940, Editions Correa, Paris, published *Trois contes de l'amour et de la mort,* an Egyptian novel that is one of Out el Kouloub's earlier works of fiction. The author's full name, Out el Kouloub el Demerdashiyya, appears on that volume as Qut-El-Kouloub. I have chosen to use Out el Kouloub, however, the author's name as it appears on all of her subsequent novels. This novel, like her others, was written in French.

I first became acquainted with the writings of Out el Kouloub in the 1970s. During that time, living in Cairo, I purchased all of her available novels, remaindered in Yvette Farazali's bookstore, Livres de France, on Kasr el Nil Street. One was missing: *Trois contes de l'amour et de la mort.* Subsequently, I searched for it but failed to located a copy for some time, even at the Library of Congress.

Before my translation of *Ramza* was published—Out el Kouloub's novel about harem life in turn of the century Egypt— I returned to Cairo and chanced to accompany my mother to the Institut Dominicain D'Etudes Orientales, in the quarter of Abbasiyya. She was visiting Père Qanawati—a monk and scholar belonging to the Dominican order—to consult on an article for the eight-volume Coptic Encyclopedia she and my father were about to publish with Macmillan.

The portly Père Qanawati received us warmly, dressed in his rope-belted, linen-white garb, his dark eyes twinkling with humor. We were ushered through massive doors into one of the sparsely furnished parlor rooms of the monastery-institute. It was a hot day.

The old tiled hallways and high-ceilinged reception rooms were cool and immaculate, havens from the dusty, noisy streets of the crowded capital. Père Qanawati offered us strong, perfectly brewed Turkish coffee accompanied by the customary, tall glass of ice-cold water. Tiny cups were brought in by an attendant in khaki work pants, a brilliantly white shirt, and an equally brilliant smile. This welcome refreshment was neatly placed on a small, polished brass tray, dented from years of use. Père Qanawati gleefully told us the latest political jokes, answered my questions about his research on alchemy, and discussed with my mother the encyclopedia article in question. Before leaving I asked if, perchance, the Institut owned any books by Out el Kouloub el Demerdashiyya. Père Qanawati beamed and led us to the library. To my surprise and delight, an assistant produced a copy of *Trois contes de l'amour et de la mort*. The good father had just performed a small feat of literary "alchemy." It is this copy of the book that I have gratefully used for my translation.

The work, comprising three poignant tales of love and death in the Egyptian countryside, had a preface, as did most of Out el Kouloub's subsequent novels, by one of a number of France's beloved writers. Many of these writers were fascinated with what they considered to be the Orient's exotic mysteries. They were also drawn to the Orient—certainly to Egypt—because of the passionate response of Egypt's aristocracy and upper classes to everything French, from language to furniture and fashion.

In a few pages of preface to Out el Kouloub's novels, such writers—usually members of the Academy Française—invariably praised her vivid characters, the veracity of her descriptions, and the ethnic resonance of her work. Unavoidably, however, they held them up to a European mirror as if only their praise could validate the novels. Their support no doubt insured the publication of these novels by such renowned French houses as Correa and Gallimard.

In his preface to *Trois contes de l'amour et de la mort*, André Maurois begins by expressing enchantment with the author's wondrous name. He writes: "Out el Kouloub (whose beauteous Arabic name means Nourishment for the Heart) is a young woman who belongs to a very old Caucasian family who came to Egypt in 1517, after the Ottoman conquest [of Egypt]. . . ."

Maurois reflects that Out el Kouloub's three tales, like the most beautiful love stories of literature, describe circumstances where "alas, love invariably leads to death." He cites Tristan and Isolde. In discussing the heroines of the novel, he further points out that "despite their veils, their Muslim education, and their harem lives, Nazira, Zariffa, and Zaheira's dramas and destinies are as profoundly felt by Europeans as are those of Manon and Carmen." He goes on to compare the stories told in this small volume to ones written by Chekhov and Turgenev. Zariffa and Ahmad, childhood sweethearts, are rent asunder by money and war; Nazira is married to a kind old merchant, but falls in love with a young jeweler and pays the price of her folly with death. Zaheira, a country girl raised with the master's children, succumbs to the charms of his handsome, European-educated son. Of the young women in *Trois contes de l'amour et de la mort,* only Zaheira escapes death, Maurois concludes, by "disarming cruel fate through resignation."

Maurois stresses that although the themes in Out el Kouloub's stories are universal, their originality and charm reside in their settings and the true ring of the author's descriptions of the life and times of her characters. Returning to a European model, however, he emphasizes that "Out el Kouloub has thoroughly assimilated the lessons of the masters. From Flaubert, she has learned to construct a story, to weight essential scenes, remaining an impassive observer of what she has created. From Anatole France, she has learned to write with simplicity, without noisy or unnecessary effects, always ending on a lyrical note." In conclusion, he confesses that the tragic stories of these "three, passionate little girls have taught me as much about Egypt as have about England, those of the young heroines of Rosamund Lehmann or Katherine Mansfield, or about France, those of Colette." [My translation of Maurois' text.]

In translating *Trois contes de l'amour et de la mort,* as well as *Ramza* (1994) and *Zanouba* (1996), I chose to omit the prefaces, instead mentioning them in passing in my translator's introductions. I considered them, at best, romantic musings of literary men swept up in fashionable waves of orientalism typical of their time, and at worst, self-indulgent and patronizing, adding little to the author's work. André Maurois' preface was of some value, however, owing to the biographical references he included about the author and her family, thus shedding some light on Out el Kouloub's past and personality.

Following is a brief, if unconfirmed, family history gleaned from Maurois's preface and a few other available sources. [See Translator's Introduction to *Zanouba* for more detail.]

Out el Kouloub el Demerdashiyya was descended from a prominent family who founded a Sufi order in Egypt, bearing their name: El Tarika el Demerdashiyya. The author's ancestor and founder of the order was Abd el Elah el Demerdash el Mohammadi, a member of the Turkish court of Sultan Kaed Bey, said to have died in 1517, the year of the family's arrival in Cairo. Generations of his descendants subsequently headed the order.

Born in 1853, Out el Kouloub's father was head of the Tarika until his death in 1930. Out el Kouloub was his only child with his second and favorite wife Zeynab Tawdeya, a woman of Moroccan-French heritage. Out el Kouloub was particularly cherished by her father, hence, perhaps, her name. Furthermore, a strong bond with her father may have contributed to Out el Kouloub's purported ease and pleasure in the company of men despite her conservative upbringing in the harem. Certainly, the convincingly rendered father-daughter relationship in her novel *Ramza,* as well as the tender grandfather-granddaughter one in the story of Zaheira, in *Trois contes de l'amour et de la mort,* suggest it. Also, her confidence in managing her vast estate and dealing with men was perhaps the result of this significant relationship with a father who was no doubt Out el Kouloub's role model.

Unfortunately, there is a paucity of information about Out el Kouloub's life, and available biographical details are sometimes conflicting. Her final years and death, particularly, are shrouded in mystery. Some have given her dates as 1892–1968 while others have cited her birth date as 1899. Some maintain that she died in Austria, others in Italy. We do know that she died in exile, having left Egypt after the family's extensive properties were seized pursuant to the 1952 revolution, which changed Egypt from a kingdom to a republic.

Out el Kouloub was educated at home from 1911 until she married in 1922. Her husband, Mustapha Mukhtar, was an attorney to the king of Egypt and a judge in the mixed tribunals. He was years her senior. The couple made their conjugal home in Alexandria, living in a magnificent villa (regrettably demolished in 1947) in the elite district of San Stephano. They had five children but divorced in 1931. Out el Kouloub was given custody of the children, an unusual decision for that time and one that diverged significantly from custom and Muslim law, whereby the father would have been favored.

After her divorce, Out el Kouloub diligently set out to further her own as well as her children's education. She is said to have studied with many distinguished members of the French Cultural Mission in Egypt and to have collected a library of more than ten thousand volumes, subsequently donated to Cairo University.

Out el Kouloub's vast land holdings—agricultural lands, orchards, and real estate—made her the richest woman of her time in Egypt. Managing these properties herself gave her experience far beyond the harem walls, while living intimately within its confines and thoroughly understanding it. Furthermore, her conjugal life in Alexandria, her knowledge of Egyptian city life, gleaned from frequent visits to a variety of Cairene neighborhoods (the quarter of the Demerdash being one, named after the family), her role as manager of a vast agricultural estate, her dealings with peasants, merchants, and "ordinary" folk, provided her with a rich mine for her writing. Like all her novels, *Trois contes de l'amour et de la mort* is abundantly interwoven with the colors, smells, sounds, popular songs, and sayings and detailed descriptions of customs and rituals of the Egypt she clearly loved. Out el Kouloub's stories are fruits of a creative imagination, as well as varied and authentic personal experiences.

While Out el Kouloub was raised in the harem, married at an early age, and throughout her life championed conservative family values, she held broad-minded political ideals, particularly in matters of equality for women. She emphatically stressed the importance of education for both sexes, inspired, no doubt, by nineteenth-century Egyptian modernists such as Sheikh Muhammad Abdu and lawyer-playwright Murqus Fahmy, as well as twentieth-century thinkers and activists like the feminist Huda Sharaawi. Out el Kouloub was certainly in agreement with Sheikh Muhammad Abdu, who argued that the development of Egypt as a nation was impeded because Muslims failed to apply the true spirit of Islam to women's lives, and with Marqus Fahmy, who stressed that Egypt would remain a backward nation so long as its womenfolk were not liberated.

Although keenly interested in Western thought and influenced by Western writings, Out el Kouloub remained nonetheless faithful to the traditional wisdoms of her native culture, particularly to Islam and its teachings. In the introduction to her novel *La nuit de la destinée,* she writes: "I traveled the world over and tasted of the most brilliant civilizations, but I never lost sight of my religious beliefs. . . . Every aspect of my life is marked by my unwavering attachment to Islam and my dedication to its teachings." [my translation]

Out el Kouloub read extensively and held a salon that drew the rich and famous from east and west and some of the best known writers and thinkers of her time, both Egyptian and European: Aziz Sidki Pasha, who became Prime Minister of Egypt; the beloved blind author, Taha Hussein; the Quranic scholar Sheikh el Maghrabi, who was her intimate friend; the French playwright, novelist, and actor, Jean Cocteau; Jean Marais, of the Comedie Française, and many others. Although most of her guests were men, some women attended such as the Egyptian feminist Mary Kahil. Adhering to the precepts of Islam, Out el Kouloub never served alcohol at these gatherings, not even for the benefit of Europeans.

In translating Out el Kouloub's novels, I have experienced the exquisite pleasures and dilemmas of manipulating language, spanning cultures, and dancing with lives to the music of words, if you will. Keeping a vigilant eye on the integrity of a story, listening carefully for overtones, staying true to the original text without denying the validity of one's own heartfelt responses to it are indeed the translator's challenge. The degree of freedom with which one approaches a translation is also crucial to its success and authenticity. This is particularly so when the author is dead and the translator must intuit her voice and her intention without her personal intervention.

My translation of *Trois contes de l'amour et de la mort,* like those of *Ramza* and *Zanouba,* is a free translation. I took the liberty, in some instances, of rearranging paragraphs whose placement I considered awkward to the fluidity of the story. Some lyrical descriptions that appeared in the middle of an action-packed scene in *Zariffa,* for example, I transferred to the beginning of the story. To this prologue

I added a few sentences to clarify the time and place and identify the listener, whom I believed to be Out el Kouloub herself: "I make frequent visits to the countryside where my family and I own large tracts of agricultural land in the fertile region of the Nile Delta. One summer night, Hagg Hassan, the aging mayor of the village called on me as was his custom. We sat quietly sipping tea at dusk. He recounted the tragedy of Zariffa and Ahmad, a tale of love and death in the Egyptian countryside around the time of the First World War. Following is the story he told me." This paragraph replaces: "Voici l'histoire de Zariffa, à peu près telle que me l'a contée, un soir, Hagg Hassan, le viel Omdeh." ("Here is Zariffa's story, more or less as it was told to me one night by Hagg Hassan, the old Omdah" [My translation]).

In working with Out el Kouloub's *Three Tales of Love and Death,* I have endeavored to smooth certain time sequences and scenes. Three such examples are the description of Sham el Nessim celebrations in *Zariffa,* the ritual of the Zar in *Nazira,* and the visit of the fortune teller in *Zaheira.* What manipulations I have effected were made particularly in an effort to keep the storyteller's voice active and spontaneous and subdue the ethnographer's pen, attempting all the while to stay true to the author's narrative. Additionally, when working with Out el Kouloub's novels, I have grappled with French as the vehicle used to portray aspects of Egyptian life and culture. This predicament provided a further challenge, specifically when conveying meanings and flavors of popular Arabic songs and sayings. These, rendered in French must keep their authenticity in yet another language, American.

I was born to an Egyptian family and lived in Egypt the first ten years of my life. Then, in the 1950's, my family moved to the United States. From 1976–87, I lived again in Egypt, both in Cairo and in the country where I built a house in the village of Shabramant, located between Giza and Saqqara.

Growing up in Egypt, speaking Arabic and French at home, becoming immersed in American language and culture from the age of ten, and returning to live in Egypt as an adult helped me negotiate some of the intricacies of this "triple-decker" translation. Of course, I have read and translated Out el Kouloub's novels through the lens of my own experiences of life and of Egypt. It is my hope, nonetheless, that this translation of *Trois contes de l'amour et de la mort*, while making stories from one culture accessible to another, succeeds in sensitvely echoing the author's voice and conveying to the reader the spirit with which she has imbued these poignant tales.

New York City   Nayra Atiya
September 1999

Zariffa and Ahmad

PROLOGUE

Night falling brings peaceful, sweet respite to the boisterous life of the countryside. Beasts of burden meander ponderously back to their stables, men and women leave the fields in groups, laughing. Children trail after them, shouting and teasing one another. The shadow of a song lingers along with the last rays of sunlight, then all grows dark and hushed.

Lantern light quivers faintly beneath the doorways of mudbrick houses. Folks gather on their stoops waiting for the moon to rise and sleep to overtake them.

I make frequent visits to the countryside where my family and I own large tracts of agricultural land in the fertile region of the Nile Delta. One summer night, Hagg Hassan, the aging mayor of the village, called on me as was his custom. We sat quietly sipping tea at dusk. He recounted the tragedy of Zariffa and Ahmad, a tale of love and death in the Egyptian countryside around the time of the First World War.

Following is the story he told me.

1 ▪ A BEDOUIN FAMILY

Zariffa was not a girl from the Nile valley, not one of our own. Although many of our girls are noted for their beauty, Zariffa's was memorable. With her proud demeanor, pure profile, and sparkling eyes, she resembled a prancing gazelle, graceful and vibrant, high strung. Her appearance gave those who saw her the impression of a light as radiant as sunlight on the desert.

One day, when I was still a young man, long ago, a caravan of Bedouins came to our village. The travelers asked permission to put up their tents, explaining that they were natives of the Fayyoum going to market from their oasis to sell young camels. The men from those parts are known for their courage and rectitude. So, as mayor of our village, I welcomed them. Our villagers made sure that they lacked for nothing; we gave them the best that our hospitality could offer. They remained three days before continuing on their way.

One day after the caravan left, one of the men returned accompanied by his wife and daughter, a child hoisted on her mother's shoulders. The little girl, Zariffa, could not have been more than two. Abdel Latif was a man of few words. His forthright manner instantly inspired trust. He explained that he had decided to leave the caravan and his brothers. He had returned to us in the hope of establishing a new life for himself and his family. He assured me that he was not running away from trouble, that he was neither a thief nor a murderer.

As the cotton-picking season was beginning, I was able to find work for him in the fields. He proved reliable and hardworking, a man of good will. For this reason, any doubts about his motives for abandoning his people were soon dispelled. He built a small house in the village. Since he never failed to lend a helping hand, he was quickly accepted and became one of us. We never did find out what could have alienated him from his people. No one ever asked. Everyone sensed that his turning his back on his past, though, had not been without great sadness.

After a day's hard work, the men used to drink tea around a fire. Abdel Latif would often talk about his native Fayyoum in ways that had us all dreaming about this mysterious place. A faraway look came into his eyes when he described his old home. He spoke softly of its abundant water, cascading streams, and lush, green fields. He spoke of hills covered in olive trees, of vineyards surrounding a green lake as big as the sea where sailboats glided quietly like great white birds.

When Abdel Latif spoke of the surrounding desert, his eyes sparkled all the more and his voice grew animated. He had spent much of his youth herding camels and sheep there. His animals had to compete for survival with wild hares and gazelles, all grazing on the sparse leaves of thorny acacia. He impressed us with stories of how Bedouins recognize the footprints of their camels from those of thousands of others no matter how far their herds stray. Sometimes, he told us, the camels wandered to the very edges of the western desert, almost to Libya. Their herders had to follow them. During one such foray Abdel Latif has met and married Zariffa's mother.

We poor Fellahin had not set foot outside our Delta village nor seen much beyond its river banks. We listened to his stories, mesmerized. We imagined that the ancient tales and legends we had grown up with must have taken place in these mysterious lands.

Although ours is a rich and fertile region, the lives we lived paled compared to the adventuresome ones our new neighbor described. We always wondered why he had given up the freedom and marvels of his former life to settle among us. However, he easily adapted, had four more children who shared our children's games and eventually worked alongside them. Zariffa, his eldest, had a special hold on everyone because of her beauty and charm. All the young men in the village were smitten.

2 ▪ AHMAD ABDOU

Zariffa's earliest playmate was named Ahmad Abdou. This son of the Delta appointed himself a knight to this desert princess. He was ever ready to protect her against teasing children. During the season when the mulberries ripened, he climbed the laden trees, filling his handkerchief with succulent fruit for her. When he was given treats—an ear of roasted corn, a sheaf of wheat grilled on an open fire, a sweet rye cake—he saved them for his Zariffa. Walking hand-in-hand into the fields of alfalfa or sitting together in the pasture or under a fragrant mimosa, they chatted endlessly. They happily shared their simple treats. Sometimes, they played at being hunters. They flopped down on their bellies, observed insects hidden among the plants. They shouted with joy when spotting a grasshopper the color of the vegetation around it. Creeping with hands cupped to capture it, they laughed when it squirmed, nipping their fingers. They took turns throwing the poor creature against a cloud of midges as if it were a valiant war horse. With a cruelty typical of children, they finished off their exhausted victim by tossing it into the irrigation ditch. They giggled watching it struggle against the current that would carry it to its death.

When Zariffa was ten or so, she began to exercise her feminine wiles on Ahmad Abdou, playing hard to get. She refused to go with him to the fields as before, preferring the company of her girlfriends and pretending to cook or bake mud pies, imitating their mothers. Like grown women, they sang provocatively and teased the boys who stood around eyeing them. Men, they sang, were not worth any more than the mud between their fingers. Already these songs spoke of seduction and of love.

Ahmad Abdou suffered Zariffa's mischievousness in silence. Being shut out of her games, he felt jealous. Yet he hung around. Zariffa had cast a spell on him with her voice, which he considered sweeter by far than the voices of her playmates. Sometimes, his impatience would get the better of him, and he would burst into the circle and pull Zariffa out by the hand, coaxing her to come sit with him beside the canal. He picked blades of grass called *filaya,* growing on the water's edge, and offered them to her. They sat teasing each other, sucking on the sweet grass.

In the month of September the whole village went out in force to harvest cotton, adults and children alike. Zariffa and Ahmad Abdou turned work into play. Their parents allowed them to pick side by side knowing that they would work faster to see who finished first. Zariffa followed Ahmad Abdou with her eyes. Her fingers were more nimble than his, and often she won. At times, however, because she cheated in order to get to the end of a row before him, she left behind some unpicked stalks. Ahmad Abdou rushed to cover for her to spare her being reprimanded.

Other times, when the overseer turned his back on the workers, some of the children, jealous of Zariffa, threw cotton balls at the girl. Ahmad Abdou, fearing that the hard seeds inside would hurt her, instantly ran to her defense, shielding Zariffa with his body and shouting down the aggressors.

More than once, Ahmad Abdou felt the sting of the overseer's stick on his shoulders because he had slowed down, dreaming about Zariffa or gazing at her graceful movements. He watched her go down the rows, bending to fill her skirt with cotton balls, her black veil floating behind her. Her singing enchanted him. Her beautiful voice brought joy to others working around her.

As Zariffa matured, her eyes shone more brightly and her breasts filled out, her small nipples pushing against the cloth of her dress. She walked erect, her body swaying like a sapling, her gait starting to resemble that of the older women around her. She applied orange henna to the palms of her hands and rubbed the heels of her feet together to make them shine alluringly. Sometimes, when she was alone, Zariffa pulled a small mirror from her pocket and admired her face. She used her mother's kohl to blacken the rims of her eyelids making her eyes seem larger. Her gaze was as soft as a gazelle's. Zariffa was aware that she was beautiful, a woman already by the age of twelve.

3 ▪ MOULED OF EL SAYYED BADAWI

The year Zariffa turned twelve, she and Ahmad Abdou attended the Mouled—the birthday of the Muslim holy man, el Sayyed Badawi. A caravan of some twenty camels carried the villagers to Tanta, where the festivities took place. Camel bridles and saddles were richly decorated with colored beads and bright tassels and pilgrims wore their finest.

The caravan started at dawn. Those staying behind wished the travelers a safe journey and made them promise to bring back gifts: prayer beads, cloth, the chick peas for which the festival was famous, sweets, and pastries. Ahmad Abdou made sure his camel was directly behind those of Zariffa and her father. She often turned to look at him, and he responded with a warm smile.

The camels moved in single file on the wide, tree-lined road bordering the canal, along the bare fields where the harvest stubble remained. As pilgrims are wont to do, the villagers burst into joyful song. Sometimes, one voice would be raised above the others, and the group would respond in chorus.

Ahmad Abdou, lulled into a dreamy state by the swaying of his camel, picked out Zariffa's voice. He listened in rapture, imagining a secret message in the words of her song:

> Oh! Sayyed Badawi
> bring my friend to sit beside me
> and I shall offer two candles up to you.
>   My friend's voice is as sweet to my ears
> as honey upon my lips.
>   His eyes touch me
> as softly as moonlight.
>   His gaze is like the first ray of light
> igniting the clouds at dawn.
>   His presence fills me with joy.
>   His warmth awakens my heart
> as the sun rising awakens the earth.

Abdel Latif was surprised by his daughter's song and asked her where she had learned it. Zariffa, giggling impishly, told him that she had heard many such songs in the village.

At five o'clock in the afternoon the caravan reached the outer limits of the town and the first sprinkling of houses. Tanta was teeming with pilgrims. Swarms of people in every sort of dress filled the streets. Some men wore fezzes, others turbans. Peasant men were dressed in new *gallabeyyas,* their colors still fresh. Peasant women wore black, their veils waving lightly in the breeze. Little girls and young women wore colorful shawls of red, orange, and yellow velveteen over brightly colored dresses. Sheikhs in majestic robes wore imposing turbans artfully wrapped about their heads. From every corner of the neighboring countryside, people had come to celebrate the holyman's glory and to visit Sayyed Badawi's mosque.

Tents were erected for visitors in the central square. Chairs were set up for notables while ordinary folk sat on the ground. The dry sound of canvas flapping in the wind filled the air. In out-of-the-way corners poorer pilgrims set up the makeshift shelters of patched blankets or quilts held up by a few sticks. Zariffa, Ahmad Abdou, and their companions were among them.

Everywhere there was the appetizing aroma of grilled meat. Hungry urchins gathered around food stands hoping to be given some tasty morsel. Ahmad Abdou and Zariffa, wide-eyed with wonder, went off exploring, hand in hand. They watched clusters of children shouting on a ferris wheel and listened to the squeals of others crowded into boat-shaped swings. They marveled at the dancers juggling chairs on their foreheads and eyed the merchandise displayed in festive booths. Oh! the lanterns, the toys, the pretty clothes, the cakes, the candies! They listened to an ambulatory drink seller clinking his castanets and announcing the virtues of his thirst-quenching drink. For a penny they happily shared a glass of his licorice water. They shared the same honey cake sold by a fat baker who wished them a future of health and happiness. Ahmad Abdou trembled, thinking he detected the taste of Zariffa's lips on the cake.

That night, Zariffa returned to her father's tent wearing a new necklace of blue beads. She showed them off along with the silk handkerchief that Ahmad Abdou had purchased for her. Everyone congratulated her. The love between the two adolescents was not a secret, of course, but Ahmad Abdou's special gift was his way of sealing their commitment. Everyone approved and looked forward to the day when the village would celebrate Ahmad and Zariffa's wedding.

The next morning was the joyful procession honoring the saint, the main event of the festivities. The celebration was noisy and no one was allowed to be somber or solemn. Even the most reserved of women and the shyest of girls let out volleys of joyous cries as the parade passed their houses. Many families waited for this blessed day to perform a son's circumcision or celebrate a wedding. In the midst of this merriment, Ahmad Abdou felt a strange sadness creep over him. The festive clamor that had elated him the night before now weighed on him. He longed to return to his village and its tranquil fields. He wanted to be alone with Zariffa, away from the frantic activity. He was uneasy watching her among all these strangers. Zariffa eyed tempting displays in the shops, listened bright-eyed to sellers hawking their wares, and cheered him up by stroking his forehead. Like all women in love, she sought to reassure him by saying, "We'll always be happy, Ahmad, as long as we love each other." She took his hand, and they joined their fellow pilgrims standing before the mosque of el Bahay, el Sayyed Badawi's beloved disciple. There, they listened to storytellers recounting the life of the master and his disciple. Everyone marveled at how el Bahay had delivered el Sayyed Badawi and his wife from the prison where they had been held captive by the invading Franks. When an imposing sheikh emerged from the mosque to head the procession, Ahmad and Zariffa giggled at the way he walked. He was weighed down by an ornate cloak, supposedly belonging to el Sayyed Badawi himself. People whispered that the spirit of the saintly man inhabited the body of this cleric. He moved as slowly and looked as wizened as if he were el Sayyed Badawi himself. He could have been a hundred years old!

As he proceeded, the sheikh was surrounded by pilgrims trying to touch the cloak, to ask for a blessing or a favor. The sick asked to be healed, the poor to grow rich, the sterile woman to conceive, the lover to be joined with his beloved. Every one wanted health and happiness. Zariffa and Ahmad wanted to touch his cloak too, but were kept back by the crowd. The young man saw this failure as a bad omen and felt apprehensive.

When the procession ended, the sheikh was hoisted up on a horse. A folk play, based on the life of el Sayyed Badawi, was enacted. Men in female dress played old women in the saint's service, while others were his companions, worn-out by battle, dressed in multicolored rags. Others were prisoners of war in chains, wearing burlap sacks, their necks caught in irons. The townspeople and merchants participating in the parade cried out their thanks to their patron saint, asking that he continue to bless them with prosperity. Students raised their voices in gratitude for the help he gave them in their studies. Even courtesans and dancing girls with garishly painted faces took part, shaking tambourines and balancing trays laden with offerings.

As a delirium seized the crowd, Ahmad Abdou took Zariffa's hand and pulled her away. They crossed a few empty streets until they reached a canal. Ahmad was motioning to a bench they could sit on when Zariffa suddenly cried out. She had lost the silk handkerchief he had given her. She burst into tears. Ahmad Abdou tenderly consoled her, telling her it didn't matter. But Zariffa would have none of it. She shook her head over and over again as tears ran down her cheeks. She knew full well the meaning of a lost handkerchief! Ahmad too knew that it was a sign of misfortune to come. He looked at Zariffa with trepidation and wondered what fate had in store for them.

4 ▪ IDYLL IN THE FIELDS

The following day the pilgrims set out early for the trek home.

Ahmad Abdou could hardly wait to get back to the village. He wanted his father, Ibrahim, to go see Abdel Latif to ask for Zariffa's hand in marriage. Ibrahim agreed, only to have Abdel Latif tell him that Ahmad was still too young. The truth was that he was less than pleased. He was sure that Zariffa, beautiful as she was, did not have to settle for the humble Ahmad Abdou. He planned to drag his feet and wait for a richer prospect for his daughter. Zariffa and Ahmad continued to meet almost daily as work in the fields often brought them together.

The winter after their trip to Tanta, they joined the villagers for the yearly orange harvest in the orchards of the pasha, the region's biggest landowner. The women and girls picked the fruit, and the men and boys loaded it into wooden crates. Squatting in the clearing at the head of the orchard, Ahmad Abdou worked in silence. Through the trees, against a bright blue sky, he could see tall, white sails quietly gliding by. As both the canal and the boats themselves were hidden from view by dense foliage, the sails seemed to be giant ploughshares, skimming the earth. The women, fleeting black silhouettes, slipped in and out the rows of young trees. Their voices, now hollering, now laughing, intoned a ballad or improvised a rhyme to tease the men. Like the dizzying perfume of orange blossom, fragments of a song hung in midair, hovered, then faded.

Now and then Zariffa ran out of the orchard with a basket of oranges on her head. She was so light on her bare feet that she seemed to skim the ground. Her young body was erect and supple and her breasts now filled out the snug bodice of her long black dress. When she looked at Ahmad Abdou, her eyelashes fluttered with pleasure, and her lips expressed her happiness with a bright smile. She stopped beside him, coyly taking the load off her head. She put her rounded arms around the basket and tipped it. The oranges rolled on the ground, some tinged with red, some golden, looking like a giant game or marbles. Then, in a flash, she was gone. As she melted into the crowd, Ahmad ached to shout out his love to her. I will never forget his spontaneous serenade, nor Zariffa's response to it. Ahmad sang:

> Hey, there! Young girl!
> You, gambooling amidst the orange trees!
> Hey there! Young girl!
> You, gambooling amidst the orange trees!
> in the sweet evening hour!
> Your beauty is more radiant than the morning sun,
> warming the banks of the Nile.
> Your gaze settles upon me like the fragrant dew
> kissing the clover at daybreak.
> My heart cherishes you, oh, my beloved!
> Willingly would I let my ears grow deaf,
> if ever they listened to words of love other than yours.
> And my eyes? I would put them out, beloved,
> if ever they dared to look at another. . . .

Ahmad's companions applauded his improvisation. From among the branches, Zariffa responded:

> My heart is yours, oh, handsome lad!
> My heart is yours, you there sitting among the winter oranges!
> Your song envelops me, young lad, like a sweet caress,
> Your song refreshes me as the night breeze rising
> cools a summer day.
> Never harm your ears, my beloved,
> for if they stopped listening
> my throat would swallow my tongue,
> and my voice would be forever silenced.
> As for your beautiful eyes, beloved,
> guard them well,
> for if they ever ceased to see me,
> I would disfigure my face
> and pray for death.

Ahmad and Zariffa were thrown together not only when working, but on holidays. On Sham el Nessim, the first day of spring, the villagers abandoned their fields for the threshing grounds and greeted the new season with singing and dancing. Only a few weeks later, with their animals, they would be toiling on the Norag, the thresher, extracting the heavy wheat kernels from their castings using the Norag's sharp, circular blades.

At sunrise on a bright spring day, the villagers formed a circle around pairs of men stick dancing. The men, calm and dignified, confronted one another, sticks poised over their heads. Their supple bodies moved artfully and spontaneously until one rival touched another. The loser stepped out silently, making way for a new competitor. Three flutes and a drum accompanied the dance. The flutes played a mournful tune to usher out the vanquished and a merry one to celebrate the victor.

Zariffa and her girlfriends stopped and watched on their way home from the canal, their water jugs still glistening and plastered with Nile grasses. Ahmad Abdou gave a shining performance. The crowd cheered his ingenious improvisations as he left the circle to join his friends. Despite the admiring looks directed at him, Ahmad had eyes only for Zariffa. Her coy glance made his heart pound. He coaxed his buddies into a ballad, a tribute to the girls:

> Dark beauties, dark beauties,
> do not envy a sultana's golden hair,
> nor wish for her skin so fair,
> for beside our own dark beauties,
> the sultana's beauty pales.
> Yes, beside our own dark beauties
> the queen appears a slave.
> Dark beauties, dark beauties,
> won't you listen to our song?
> Won't you gently, won't you sweetly,
> welcome our words of love? . . .

Zariffa and her girlfriends replied in chorus:

> Young lads, young lads
> calling us with your song,
> you are the date palms, straight and strong
> We the fragrant flowers

> listening to that song
> calling us, calling us . . .
>
> You are the date palms
> proud and strong
> We the song birds
> resting, resting
> in your sheltering fronds . . .

As the sun set, their voices trailed off and the festivities ended. The young men would down their sparring, and the young women strolled home to take up their evening chores.

5 ▪ MABROUK EL GABALI

After a time, Abdel Latif began to feel pressured by Ahmad Abdou's ardent wooing of Zariffa. He told Ahmad that their frequent meetings must stop—they were no longer children innocently playing. He began to monitor his daughter's comings and goings.

Ahmad Abdou grew despondent, lost his appetite, and began wasting away. His family became impatient and complained. He lay about at home, wandered aimlessly, and stopped working. They were short of money and needed his income. They had to give up eating meat and missed the roasted lamb they feasted on every Tuesday. Only his father understood Ahmad's pain.

One day Ibrahim decided to visit Abdel Latif to plead Ahmad's case. He took with him several village notables. Zariffa's father was flattered. He ushered in his callers with great courtesy, pressed cup upon cup of coffee upon them, but promised nothing. Abdel Latif was not a man to give in without first driving a hard bargain.

Meanwhile Ibrahim tried to distract Ahmad by taking him along to market to sell one of their calves. Ahmad went but remained indifferent to all the excitement: the merry clink of the water bearer's castanets, the loud calls of the vegetable hawkers, the gossip of the poultry vendors . . . In fact, he felt dazed and defeated. When an acquaintance greeted him, he answered absentmindedly. Nothing brought him relief.

Meanwhile, Ibrahim was waiting patiently for a buyer. Sitting near a carpenter's shop, he watched as the man laboriously cut a stout beam. How hard it was! Much like life. Suddenly he spied Mabrouk el Gabali, a Bedouin chieftain feared throughout lower Egypt. Sheikh Mabrouk had been his benefactor when Ibrahim was only a lad. Ibrahim instantly thought that the chieftain, who still held him in affection, might be able to help.

The stories told about Mabrouk el Gabali's ancestors had become the stuff of legends. Ordinary folk and even rulers were in awe of the Gabali clan. The khedive himself had met with Sheikh Mabrouk, who had not even averted his eyes in the presence of Effendina! It was reported that should their swords fail them, these tribesmen would sink their teeth into an enemy's neck, instantly killing him. Rumors ran wild that Mabrouk's clansmen raided villages, capturing women who subsequently protested their innocence but secretly relished the vigor and power of their assailants. As a boy Ibrahim had herded sheep for Sheikh Mabrouk. He remembered his carefree life in the desert and the sheikh's many kindnesses to him.

Ibrahim eagerly rose to greet his old master and confided his torment. He asked him to intervene on behalf of his son and described Abdel Latif's pride and his refusal to promise Zariffa's hand to his boy. He explained that they had been childhood sweethearts, devoted to one another. Sheikh Mabrouk agreed to help.

One night, soon after that encounter, the villagers were startled by the distant rumble of galloping hooves. They pricked up their ears, murmuring that thieves must be heading for the village. The most fearful locked the doors to their houses; the rich made sure their money was securely hidden. Not so for Ibrahim and his family, who had been forewarned of Mabrouk el Gabali's visit. Having waited for this signal, father and son went to meet their guests, each carrying a calf. When the Bedouin chieftain and his clansmen finally appeared, Ibrahim slaughtered the animals to honor and welcome them. The horses snorted and stamped their feet in the bloody puddles. Reassured by Ibrahim that no danger was at hand, children excitedly swarmed around the horsemen, who were regally draped in white shawls.

Sheikh Mabrouk exchanged a formal greeting with Ibrahim and asked him to lead him to Abdel Latif's house. Zariffa's father puffed up with pride to welcome such an imposing visitor. He donned his best *gallabiyya,* shouted for a fire to be lighted and coffee to be prepared, and borrowed lanterns from his neighbors to illuminate the house. Ibrahim introduced Mabrouk el Gabali. All those gathered respectfully kissed the chieftain's hand. Sheikh Mabrouk exchanged courtesies and lengthy compliments with his host, and the men shook hands. Someone covered their clasped right hands with a handkerchief as the chieftain recited the opening verse from the Quran to bless the meeting. Finally, he addressed his host. In a solemn voice Sheikh Mabrouk declared: "Your daughter, Abdel Latif, is as my own, and Ibrahim's son is as my son. I am here to unite my son and daughter in matrimony. Such is my wish and God's will."

Zariffa's father could not deny Mabrouk el Gabali's request. To do so would have been considered an affront; Abdel Latif would have had to offer a gift of forty camels to the Gabali clan to make amends. He could neither afford to put himself in their bad graces nor pay the penalty for absolution. So he agreed. Not only that, but he felt dutybound to declare that this union had been his most cherished wish. He was deeply honored by this mark of respect accorded his family, he told Sheikh Mabrouk. Furthermore, in order for his "happiness" to be complete, his honored guest must preside over the signing of the marriage contract. The chieftain accepted, and the ceremony was set a few days hence. Moments later, the horsemen departed the village as suddenly as they had come, returning to the wide-open spaces of the desert.

6 ▪ ENGAGEMENT

Happiness followed sorrow. Ahmad Abdou regained his smile and with it his voice. He sang:

> Oh, rejoice my heart!
> Rejoice my heart!
> Soon my beloved and I shall be one.

> Soon my arms will hold her.
> Rejoice my heart, rejoice!
> Soon we shall embrace.
> Soon I will sip honey
> from the lips of my beloved . . .

At dawn on the day after the chieftain's visit, Ibrahim and his wife went to a nearby market to purchase gifts for Zariffa. That same afternoon, at the hour when the peasants and their animals quit the fields, twelve women left the bridegroom's house for the bride's. On their heads they carried large copper trays laden with gifts: rice, sugar, tea, henna, soap, headscarves, a stout pair of shoes, fabric for dresses, and a bright velveteen shawl. Young girls accompanied them, dressed in their best, their hair freshly washed, their tresses draped alluringly over one shoulder. Veils fluttered in the breeze, long dresses swept the dusty road, obliterating the women's footsteps.

They sang:

> I am the sesame seed my beloved
> scatters to the birds,
> and the honey he longs to taste.
> He is the vessel waiting for my sweet nectar,
> I am the honey he longs to taste.
> At dusk, when my lips touch his,
> his eyes meet mine in a tender caress. . . .
> Oh, beloved! In your embrace,
> Oh, beloved! In your embrace,
> I will learn the delights of heaven. . . .

Singing and clapping, the women moved in procession, joined by neighbors along the way. Before Zariffa's house, they filled the air with their joyous cries, to which the bride's mother and aunts responded with resounding ululations.

Zariffa, decked out in her finest, sat beaming in the courtyard. Eyes sparkling, she eyed the gifts before the trays were covered with crimson tulle. They would remain on display for fifteen days, a period during which the bride was not to set foot outside her house.

That same night, Ahmad Abdou's father and uncles called on Abdel Latif. Zariffa's father awaited them with male members of his family. Sitting in a circle on the ground that had been freshly covered with wood shavings, they shared greetings, compliments, and a water pipe. The conversation was solemn. Everyone took turns singing the praises of the bride, the groom, and their families after which negotiations began.

Ahmad Abdou's father placed twenty-five gold pieces, twenty-five guineas, before Abdel Latif. The bride's father was not satisfied. Bargaining ensued, sometimes everyone speaking at once. Ibrahim offered another fifteen guineas to be paid later as an "after" dowry. Abdel Latif accepted, but he had additional requirements. Once a week, Zariffa must be allowed to have the milk from the family cow and the eggs laid by their chickens for her own use. Ibrahim's family revolted. What would Ibrahim feed his family on that day? Abdel Latif, knowing he had the upper hand, stood fast, adding that Zariffa must also be spared work in the fields during the first six months of marriage. Ibrahim conceded even this, knowing how desperate Ahmad was. Finally, all was agreed. Despite Ibrahim's displeasure with Abdel Latif's terms, the men exchanged more formal compliments and good wishes, parting on a cordial note.

That very same night, the crimson tulle covering the bridal gifts mysteriously caught fire. Zariffa's mother put it out instantly but took it as a terrible omen. When Ahmad heard about the accident, he became apprehensive again, until the young men gathered to celebrate his happiness reassured him. Accompanied by flutes and drums, they coaxed Ahmad to join in singing a traditional ballad:

> On my bride's cheeks, a thousand rosebuds bloom.
> A thousand roses adorn the cheeks of my beloved.
> No lips have touched her cheeks,
> mine will be the first,
> mine will be the first.
> Gazing at my beloved, I declare:
> "Do not fear my love, oh delicate virgin!
> I shall come to you as gently as the dew.
> settling on the flowers at dawn . . ."
> On my bride's cheeks a thousand rosebuds bloom.
> A thousand roses adorn the cheeks of my beloved. . . .

7 ▪ TEARS AND KISSES

Eleven days passed in continuous celebration. On the twelfth day, however, tragedy struck. Zariffa's brother was irrigating his field one night when a neighbor accused him of taking all the water for himself. The accusation triggered an argument during which the irate neighbor called Zariffa's brother a foreigner, alluding to his father's origins outside the village. The two came to violent blows. By the time the peasants in the neighboring fields rushed to separate them, it was too late. Zariffa's brother lay dead, his head bleeding. He was carried home just as the young bride donned her wedding dress. She was showing off and bantering with her friends when she heard her mother scream.

When Zariffa's mother saw her son dead, she threw herself on his body and wailed. In despair, she tore at her clothing and hair and heaped dust upon her head. Zariffa began to wail too and yanked off her wedding dress. She raced around like a madwoman. In her grief, she grabbed the blueing from the laundry tub and smeared her face.

Fate was conspiring against Zariffa. She had just lost a brother. Next, she would lose her beloved bridegroom. No wedding could take place in the wake of such a tragedy. She would have to wait a full year, the ritual year of mourning. Farewell to joyous celebration! Farewell to sweet love songs! Farewell to the life she and Ahmad had longed for since childhood! Zariffa continued weeping and wondered what other misfortunes lay in wait for her.

When Ahmad heard the news, he felt as if the earth had suddenly opened up and swallowed him. Had he not had premonitions of calamity all along? Sensitive as he was, he was quickly thrown back into the depths of depression. His family tried to console him, but to no avail. Every evening, he set out for the canal, hoping for a glimpse of Zariffa. Although she was not allowed to speak to him, she smiled sadly. That smile was his only solace. Once, when Zariffa failed to come at the usual hour, Ahmad felt his heart would break. Twilight crept up and the banks of the canal became deserted as everyone started home. Ahmad waited. Finally, Zariffa did appear. Ahmad watched her intently as she approached. His heart pounded, his eyes drank in the graceful arc of her young body, her slender neck and sweet face, so pale above the black dress she was wearing. He was almost close enough to touch her. He ached to hold her. He longed to speak . . . Standing in the shadows, a thought suddenly flashed into his mind: Why not throw himself upon Zariffa, grab her . . . Instantly, he shuddered with disgust. "Am I a savage beast? A thief out to steal kisses?!" Zariffa saw him blanch and broke the silence: "What's wrong, Ahmad?" He told her only that he was suddenly thirsty. "Let me drink from your hands, Zariffa," he murmured. Zariffa smiled. Cupping her hands, she scooped water from the canal. The water shimmered. Ahmad felt dizzy. He plunged his face into Zariffa's waiting hands. When he looked up, her eyes were upon him. He gently took her head between his hands, and stroking her face, he kissed her. Zariffa, loving him as much as he loved her, melted into his arms. Both sighed in wonder. To what land of enchantment had they suddenly been transported?

When it began to grow dark they knew they must leave. They agreed to meet every evening. The deserted banks of this canal, which had silently witnessed their first kiss, would become their secret home.

8 ▪ THE WAR

One day, a group of young men returned home to the village from Cairo. They had been sent to the capital to study at Al Azhar University and had just graduated. They strutted about, proud of the turbans they could now wear to indicate their learning and their status. They were clerics in a village of illiterate peasants, and everyone treated them with respect. They brought news of the big city at a time when villages had few means of communication. They also brought news of the world. Cairo hotels were being used as hospitals and were full of English soldiers who had been wounded in a war in Europe. Not only was all of Europe at war, but the fighting had reached Suez. Battles were being waged on the very banks of the canal that some of the old timers had been forced to dig.

Mansour was the proudest of these young Azharites, as his family was one of the richest in the village. He declared himself their spokesman, proclaiming that Allah's wrath has been aroused. The British dogs hadn't just occupied Egypt; they had forced native recruits to fight against their Muslim brothers, the Turks. And to make matters worse, they had banished the Khedive Abbas! "They're now masters of the land!" cried Mansour. "No good will come of that!" A sheikh from Al Azhar had even had a divine revelation: seven years of famine would soon plague Egypt. Rich city dwellers were hoarding provisions, filling their storerooms with wheat, corn, beans . . . Full of newfound dignity, Mansour urged his fellow villagers to do the same.

One day the young cleric saw Zariffa in the courtyard of her father's house. She was feeding her cow a handful of clover. She looked as fresh as a field of flowers. He was instantly smitten and resolved to ask for her hand in marriage. When he discovered that she was betrothed to Ahmad Abdou, Mansour began to scheme. He would find a way to remove his humble rival!

At the time, the British forces had begun to comb the countryside for recruits, able-bodied men to build a railroad in the desert. When only three men from the village volunteered, it was declared that the rest would have to be drafted. Mansour saw his chance. Using his influence, he made sure that Ahmad Abdou was among those called and shipped off to training camps in Cairo.

On the eve of Ahmad's departure the lovers sat on the banks of the canal one last time. They affirmed their undying devotion to one another. Ahmad whispered: "You know that I'll never forget you, Zariffa. Your picture will be etched on my heart, even if I'm sent to the ends of the earth, my beloved. If I have to be away from you for the rest of my life, you would still be all I would think about . . . I'll miss seeing you every night, and I'll miss your kisses . . ."

Zariffa struggled to keep up her courage. Speaking softly, she declared: "Every night, my beloved, I'll return to this place and feel your presence here. Oh, Ahmad, I'll see your face reflected in the water and ask the moon to talk to me about you . . . She'll be looking down on both of us . . . Oh, Ahmad, I'll stay home like a faithful wife waiting for her husband. At night you will come to me in my dreams and share my sleep, beloved . . ."

Finally, when Ahmad and Zariffa had to part, she put her face against his shoulder. They were both weeping. As they embraced the salt of their tears mingled with their kisses.

Although Zariffa returned home late, no one reprimanded her. Not even her father uttered a word since he couldn't ignore the resolute set of her jaw or the fierce look of pain in her eyes.

In the months that followed, three letters from Ahmad arrived addressed to his father. These sparse missives had been dictated to a scribe who took it upon himself to embellish the illiterate peasant's words with flowery greetings. As Ibrahim could not read, Mansour was called upon. Of course, he was only too pleased to oblige since he knew Zariffa would run to listen. He showed off and paraded before the young woman in his handsome sheikh's robes. He was convinced that Zariffa would soon forget Ahmad. How could she resist him!

Ahmad's first letter was sent from Cairo, from a training camp in Roda. The second came from a British encampment in Kantara, on the Suez canal. He reported that he had been vaccinated, issued a soldier's yellow uniform, and that he and his mates were forced to take part in military exercises.

Three weeks later his third and last letter, dated August 1916, arrived from Sinai. His company was putting down a railroad. Everyone was suffering from the extreme heat in the desert, fatigued and badly nourished. He added that he could not get used to the constant bombardments and that everyone was homesick. He sounded sad and discouraged.

Zariffa worried and wept. Every evening she faithfully returned to the banks of the canal as if she were going on a pilgrimage. Only there, at the water's edge, could she unburden her heart. As soon as she was alone, she addressed her absent lover: "My Ahmad, do you still love me as much as I love you? I wonder . . . Do you know that you are my one and only love? Am I as present in your dreams as you are in mine? Oh, Ahmad, you know that you're the light of my eyes, the only song my heart sings! I weep with each sunrise and sunset, my beloved, and not a day goes by that I don't plead with the passing breeze to drink my tears and carry them to you. These are my love letters . . . Will you ever get them? Are you too far away? Without you, my beloved, I'm nothing but a poor, lost soul! Will you always remember me? Will time sweep away my image from your mind? Will it erase me from your heart like the wind has erased our footprints beside the canal?"

Zariffa spoke thus and wept.

9 ▪ A FATHER'S CRUELTY

Meanwhile, the village continued along its plodding course, guided by the rhythm of the seasons. At harvest time, the laughter of boys and girls rang out as the cotton and wheat fields yielded yet another crop. Zariffa's voice, however, was not among them. She worked in silence, ignoring Mansour, who courted her every chance he got. Mansour had begun to shower her family with gifts, sending crates of early oranges, bringing pocket mirrors or colorful headscarves for the little girls, penny whistles for the little boys. His mother supported his suit through frequent visits to Zariffa's mother, a sign of the family's serious intentions. Zariffa's mother was flattered by the attention and reciprocated. Together, the two mothers paid their respects to the dead. They visited the cemetery with flowers and food, spending the day there, gossiping and discussing their children. They shared sweets and cakes they had made for one another. Om Mansour confessed that she wanted to see her son wed. Oh, if only he could find a bride like the beautiful Zariffa!

Mansour's father also did his part. He praised Abdel Latif's good sense and prudence, calling upon him to join the village notables to settle a dispute or mediate a conflict over water rights. He threw business opportunities in Abdel Latif's direction, earning him more money than he could make in a month of arduous labor in the fields. Abdel Latif began to act superior. He wore a new blue *gallabiyya* fashioned from the best cloth on the market, bought tan leather shoes for his usually bare feet, and increased the size of his turban as a mark of his newfound distinction. He was clearly pleased with his good luck. Only Zariffa remained indifferent.

One bright morning, as the first rays of the sun glimmered upon the canal and dew drops still trembled on the clover, Zariffa received tragic news. She was harvesting clover for her cow when her youngest sister, Mbarka, ran toward her, shouting and crying: "Zariffa, Zariffa! Mohammed Abdel Rabous and Moustafa Sayyed are back from the war! They're telling everyone that Ahmad Abdou is dead!"

I was inspecting an irrigation ditch when I heard Zariffa's blood-curdling scream and saw her take off like a flash in the direction of the village. I rushed after her. She grabbed Moustafa Sayyed, who was in the village square, in the middle of a crowd. Zariffa had elbowed her way to him, shouting, "What's happened to Ahmad? What's happened to Ahmad?" The young soldier repeated the story he had told the others: The company was digging a trench. A sandstorm was brewing. The Turks staged a surprise attack. Everyone scattered. When they returned to their tents, Ahmad Abdou was missing. Some said he was hit by a stray bullet. Others said he got lost, buried in the swirling sands. Most thought he must be dead. One thing was certain, Ahmad had disappeared in that faraway desert.

Zariffa listened in shock. The women around her began to wail. She could not utter a sound. She had turned to stone. Mansour came toward her. When he offered his condolences, Zariffa spun around and bolted. She went to Ahmad Abdou's house where she collapsed, sobbing with his mother. All that day, their wails were heart rending!

Zariffa was inconsolable. Slowly, she wasted away. She refused to speak to anyone and hardly ate. Her father tried to distract her from her grief, but in vain. Never having been partial to Ahmad Abdou, he couldn't help seeing opportunity in the midst of misfortune. Zariffa could marry a rich man. Not only that, but the war had driven up the price of cotton, bringing Abdel Latif unexpected prosperity. Yet, he was not indifferent to his daughter's unhappiness. As a father, he felt he had her best interest at heart. She was young and beautiful. She would soon forget Ahmad. To distract her, he took her to Cairo to visit some saints' tombs. She would drink the blessed water from Sheikh Golshani's well, which was reputed to heal the lovesick. But nothing helped Zariffa. She remained withdrawn and melancholy.

Finally, Mansour's father intervened. God works in mysterious ways, he told Abdel Latif. Who are we to question his infinite wisdom? Perhaps marriage would cure Zariffa of her dejection. His son was standing ready. Given Zariffa's beauty and sweet disposition, he was offering her a generous dowry: one hundred guineas. In those days, one hundred guineas could buy a sizable chunk of the richest agricultural land in the area! Abdel Latif was dazzled. Mansour was not only rich, but educated. He was a man of the cloth. He was not a peasant but a sheikh. He knew the blessed Quran by heart from cover to cover. He had a beautiful voice and chanted every verse without faltering! What more could a girl want?!

Abdel Latif hurried to tell his wife the news. The good woman warned her husband that it was too soon. Zariffa would take his offer of marriage as a violation of Ahmad's sacred memory.

Abdel Latif would not listen: "Zariffa can't refuse! I won't let her ruin her life! I'll know how to make her accept. Even the hardest ground can be plowed if you know how. I'll beat some sense into her if she won't listen to reason! One day, your daughter will thank me . . ."

Zariffa's mother tried to protest. He would have none of it. He exclaimed: "Have you gone mad, woman? We can't pass up this opportunity! Just think of the house she'll live in, the silk frocks she'll have, the rich meals she'll eat! Why, she can have meat every day of the week, even twice a day, dip her fingers in cream morning, noon and night! . . ."

Zariffa's mother said no more. She thought of Ahmad's family, though, fearing his mother's curse.

Finally, she persuaded Abdel Latif to delay until Ahmad's mother went to her widowed sister's in the next village. With Om Ahmad gone, Zariffa would not be able to hide under her wing as she had done since the tragedy. She would not be constantly reminded of Ahmad, talking incessantly about him with his mother. Abdel Latif agreed to humor her, but met with Mansour's father to negotiate.

One evening, not long after Ahmad's mother had departed, Mansour's mother started for Zariffa's house bearing gifts. To appear to advantage and give herself an alluringly full figure, Om Mansour wore all her dresses at once and draped her black veil majestically about her. Her thick gold ankle rings clinked seductively as she walked. The males in her family fired celebratory shots, and the women ululated. Everyone envied Zariffa, forgetting her grief.

Zariffa, returning from the canal, instantly guessed the reason for the commotion. Her face was livid. She yelled, "I'll never marry Mansour! I'll never marry Mansour or anyone else!" When Abdel

Latif came at her, cursing and threatening, she ran away. At a spot where the river meets the canal, she was trapped and promptly threw herself into the water. A neighbor leapt in after her and brought her back to shore, dripping and distraught.

Abdel Latif was enraged and commenced to beat his daughter until some of his neighbors dragged him away. Zariffa wept hysterically, rolling on the ground, tearing her clothing, covering her face with mud. She pleaded with Abdel Latif, crying, "Oh! father! Keep me with you! Keep me at home! I'll be your humble servant for the rest of my days! Don't make me marry Mansour! I don't want to marry Mansour! I know Ahmad's coming back! I know he's coming back! He came to me in a dream! Ahmad's not dead! He's not dead! He's not dead!"

Abdel Latif had made his decision. Nothing would change his mind, not even his daughter's pathetic pleas and tears. He dragged Zariffa home, gave her another hiding, and locked her up.

10 ▪ THE WEDDING

A few days after the scene at the river, the father of the bride and the father of the groom signed the marriage contract before a judge and a handful of guests. Abdel Latif had invited all of his neighbors as well as a few merchants of his acquaintance from nearby villages.

While the bride was being given a ritual bath by the womenfolk, a colorful tent was erected beside the house for the men. The courtyard had been cleared of farming tools and mounds of the dried twigs gathered for fuel at the close of each corn and cotton harvest. Older women dressed in black and girls in colorful frocks, their hair freshly washed and oiled to a shine, milled about in the courtyard. The company made such a ruckus that Zariffa's pigeons flew off to neighboring rooftops. Chickens, however, bolder by nature, continued to scratch for food and peck at the ground, nervously darting in and out among the guests.

Upstairs, in her room, the bride wept bitterly. Everyone knew that she had been beaten into submission. Some of the women declared that it was for her own good. The village crones, however, shook their heads and muttered that no good would come of such a marriage, no matter how rich the bridegroom and generous the dowry.

A few minutes before sunset, when Zariffa appeared, a murmur rose among the guests. She was wearing a long pink dress that made her pale face and burning eyes appear even more poignant. Her mother placed the traditional crimson shawl upon her head. The village bather came forward to wash her feet, keeping a trained eye on the silver coins tossed into the basin, her reward. Zariffa did as she was told, but her entire being sickened at the thought of surrendering her body to anyone but Ahmad. She felt like a beast being lead to slaughter and secretly vowed that Mansour would never have her heart.

Meanwhile, at the groom's house, preparations were in full swing. There was singing, laughter, noisy greetings, and a running exchange of good wishes. Mansour beamed, dreaming of the moment he would possess the gazelle he so ardently desired. Four of his closest friends teased him as they slathered henna on the bridegroom's hands and feet, turning them a festive orange. The village barber (always present at these affairs) shaved him, rubbed his head with a damp towel, and shouted: "May all those who wish health and happiness to the groom reward the barber!" A volley of coins were tossed in his direction.

As it was a custom to circumcise boys at the time of weddings, Mansour's ten-year-old nephew, Hanafi, was brought in. Putting him on his uncle's knees, the barber first cut a swatch of the little boy's hair and presented it to the groom for good luck before proceeding with the operation. He was generously rewarded.

Gradually, makeshift bands began to form. The guests clapped, banged on pots and pans and bottles, and sang wedding songs meant to welcome a bride to her bridegroom's clan:

> Oh land of my people
> Welcome my betrothed to your valley
> Welcome my beloved to your shores
> Welcome her to where the Nile is limitless
> Welcome her to where the river is as wide as the sea . . .

Little boys tied scarves around their hips and danced, swaying suggestively. They stuffed rags into their *gallabiyya*s, pretending to have breasts and bellies, mimicking their pregnant mothers and sisters. They grimaced, joked, clapped, and strutted around to the amusement of the company. Everyone laughed and teased the bridegroom, finally wishing him long life, happiness, prosperity, and a numerous progeny.

The next day, in the early afternoon, Zariffa was groomed for her wedding night. Abdel Latif had threatened her with blows if she put up any fuss. But Zariffa was too heartbroken to resist. She did not even wince when the hair on her body was plucked out before her bridal bath. When her skin had been rubbed with jasmine-scented oil, her mother dressed her in the five gowns prepared for the occasion. Layered one on top of the other, they were an indication of her new status, as was the dazzling gold jewelry, her father-in-law's gift, the *shabka*. Earrings, bracelets, and ankle rings as well as an elaborate pectoral necklace with little crescent moons and hanging coins completed her outfit. The necklace would have once delighted Zariffa but not now. At last, when a white veil and the crimson shawl were placed upon her head and face, she was led out.

Suffocated by the weight of her clothing and jewelry, Zariffa could hardly walk. In the courtyard her knees buckled. Her mother and aunts let her sit down again while the women intoned the virgin's serenade:

> Oh! light of your father's house
> Still so young, soon to be a bride
> Welcome to your bridegroom's house.
> Oh! light of your mother's eyes
> don your father-in-law's gifts,
> jewelry of pure gold to match your golden beauty.
> Oh! light of your bridegroom's heart,
> your face pure as the rising summer moon,
> your arms smooth as winter butter,
> your feet clean as fresh-drawn milk in spring,
> step lightly, oh virgin, step lightly
> upon the rich bridal carpet,
> put down to shield your feet from dust,
> your bridegroom's gift of welcome . . .

Zariffa, exhausted, nodded. As the voices reached a crescendo, however, she was startled by a sudden apparition. She saw soldiers marching in single file to the beat of a drum and the sound of a flute. Ahmad Abdou was at their head. She cried out once and fainted. The singing stopped. The women rushed to her side. Someone cut an onion and passed it under her nose, beneath the crimson shawl. Zariffa came to, sobbing.

It was getting late. Abdel Latif was growing impatient. A camel knelt at the door, waiting to carry the bride to the bridegroom's house. The wooden saddle was decorated with feathers and multicolored ribbons, branches, and flowers. Abdel Latif took Zariffa from the women, lifting her into the saddle. The wedding procession began to move, circling the village three times. The camel was followed by a young buffalo and two small donkeys carrying sacks of wheat, corn, and oats. Abdel Latif was flanked by his youngest daughters, carrying gifts of honey and clarified butter for the bridegroom's mother. To the right and left of the bride, young men showed off on prancing horses.

Earlier, Mansour had taken the same route, serenaded by his friends and the men in his family, stopping at a holy man's mausoleum to pray and receive a blessing.

When Zariffa arrived, he was waiting expectantly. His father welcomed the bride with formal words of greeting. Lifting her down from the saddle, he carried her to the house. Her mother-in-law barred the door waiting for Zariffa to crawl past her in a show of submission. When she led her to the nuptial chamber, the bridegroom and his sisters took over.

Zariffa performed these traditional rituals as if in a dream whose very substance was pain. When the women uncovered her face, she looked so pale and drawn that the joyous cries momentarily froze upon their lips. Without a word, they pushed her down. Mansour accomplished his mission. Zariffa's cry of pain was lost in a sea of shrill ululations. Minutes later, a bloodied sheet was hoisted up before the guests, a sign of the bride's virginity. Family honor had been safeguarded. Everyone cheered, the women ululated and danced. Zariffa's mother wrapped the bloodied sheet around her head and beamed with pride.

Through her tears, Zariffa stared at the faces of her new sisters-in-law. Silently, she called her beloved to come to her rescue, imploring the ghostly shadow of Ahmad Abdou not to abandon her in her hour of need.

11 ▪ THE RETURNED

O ne summer afternoon the heat descended with crushing might upon the dozing village. The fields and dusty roads were deserted. The fat village grocer, Sitt Om Youssef, was slumped in her dilapidated chair, fast asleep. Hoards of flies buzzed on the countertop. Two sparrows pecked undisturbed at a sugarloaf. Om Youssef was suddenly startled awake by a noise and a sudden apparition. Silhouetted in her doorway stood a disheveled, bearded man, covered in rags, his bare feet caked with mud. The old woman gasped, "Ya, Allah! Ya, Allah!" Was it Ahmad Abdou?! Were her eyes playing tricks on her? Ahmad Abdou was dead . . .

Ahmad Abdou spoke up. He was not a ghost. He told Om Youssef his tale of woe: He had been taken prisoner by the Turks and shipped off to a camp in Aleppo. When the war ended he began his long trek home to the village. Ahmad hastened to ask after his parents, Zariffa . . . Sitt Om Youssef did not dare tell him about the wedding, answering only that everyone was in good health. As soon as he hobbled away, she rushed to her neighbors with the news.

In the courtyard of her husband's house, Zariffa sat brooding. A month had elapsed since her marriage. She had been ill, hanging by a thread between life and death. A doctor, called in from the nearby town, could not understand what ailed her. She was improving but had become a shadow of herself. Where was the Zariffa whose singing had brought joy to her companions working in the orchards and the fields?! She looked to housework to distract her from her sorrow and did her share of the family's baking. But she remained melancholy, neither joining in the women's songs nor their chatter. She was often lost in thought, watching chickens scratch for grain, cattle, donkeys, camels, sheep going past . . . She listened numbly to the cocks crowing at daybreak and was even seen to smile at the neighbor's goat scampering up the side of a wall to reach the tasty green leaves of an overhanging tree.

An unyielding sun descended on the open courtyard. The sky was a shimmering blue. Zariffa looked up and sighed, unsettled. She had not left Mansour's house since her wedding day. Would she ever again see the canal that had witnessed her vows and Ahmad's? Their first kiss and sad farewell?

She lived in the house of a rich man, yet she was oblivious to its comforts. She was spared work in the fields, yet she would have welcomed it. Her father-in-law had dug a well to save her the toil of fetching water, but she missed the sound of the wavelets lapping at the banks of the canal. Instead, she had to listen to the plaintive creaking of the chain pulling water from the well and remain cloistered.

What was the use of this abundance when the price was marriage to a man she despised? Would it bring back her lost love? She did not even have the consolation of visiting her beloved's grave! Zariffa's eyes filled. She was tormented. She murmured, "Better dead, beloved Ahmad, than alive to see your Zariffa forced into another's arms!" Tears of shame overwhelmed her.

All at once a neighbor burst into the courtyard. The women stopped their work, which was piling fresh loaves into hampers. They questioned her, and she gushed: "Ahmad Abdou's alive! He was taken prisoner! He's just come home! Om Youssef saw him . . ."

Hearing this news, Zariffa screamed and collapsed. Her sisters-in-law rushed to her side, splashing her face with water, calling her name, fanning her, but to no avail. Zariffa was dead.

The tragic news spread quickly, plunging the village into grief once again. Zariffa's mother came running. She wailed, tore her clothes in despair, and cursed the day she had lived to see her daughter's ill-fated marriage. Mansour followed on her heels and threw himself upon Zariffa's body, sobbing. In his way, he had loved her!

When Ahmad Abdou learned that Zariffa was not only married but had just dropped dead, he went crazy. He fled to the fields, disappearing before anyone could stop him.

12 ▪ THE BURIAL

Oh! tragic day! The village fell into another spell of gloom when Zariffa died. The women lamented, their strident wails carrying all the way to the fields: "Houuuh, Houuuh, Houuuh."

Children clung to their mothers' skirts, hardly daring to utter a word, much less go out and play. Everyone was in shock.

That night a group of men went from village to village sounding the death drum, announcing a funeral would take place. A party was formed to search for Ahmad. On the worn footpaths and dusty roads, Ahmad Abdou's father, accompanied by a few men, carried torches and shouted his name, but there was no answer. Ibrahim, distraught, had mourned his son, found him and lost him again. He insisted on dragging the canal for the boy's body, but to no avail. Ahmad remained missing.

At home, Zariffa's body was laid on a platform freshly strewn with wood shavings. Her face was covered with her wedding veil, but her mother refused to dress her in her wedding gown. Her beautiful hair hung loose. Little by little the room filled with black-clad mourners. Some wailed and wept over Zariffa's untimely death, some over their own troubles. Hired weepers lamented:

Oh, black-eyed gazelle, you have closed your eyes too soon, too soon
Oh, good people!
Can you fathom the majestic date palm felled before it bears fruit?
Or imagine the grass mown while still wet with dew?
Oh, good people!
Can you fathom the flower cut while still in bud?
Or imagine the maiden taken in the spring of life?
Oh, black-eyed gazelle, you have left too soon,
too soon . . .

In their pens, cattle stamped, and the sheep bleated. Pigeons beat their wings incessantly, and the dogs barked. As the moon rose, the village kept vigil. Too much had happened in a short few months. Everyone felt the somber weight of misfortune.

Abdel Latif mourned the passing of his daughter, saying he had killed her. Mansour grieved silently, no longer allowed to look at his wife's face now that death had taken possession of her.

At midnight, the mourners and hired weepers trickled out. Mansour's mother wondered at the calamity that had befallen them. Why had God in his infinite wisdom seen fit to snatch her son's bride so soon! Zariffa's mother wept quietly now, sitting beside her daughter's body. A small lamp was burning. Zariffa looked peaceful at last. As the shadows deepened, angels took possession of her soul.

We wondered about Ahmad Abdou. Was he hiding? Was he dead or alive? In his demented state, he was capable of anything. Was he searching for Zariffa along the footpaths they had walked together? Was he looking for her in the stars? All night, his relatives called him, but he never responded.

At dawn the men went about their business, and the women milked their cows. Then, everyone gathered at Mansour's house. While the men remained outside reciting verses from the Quran, the women prepared to wash the body. Zariffa's mother, hysterical with grief, threw herself upon her daughter's body, weeping. She was quickly yanked off and reminded that tears falling on the body before the ritual bath were a sacrilege. When they had calmed her, the women placed Zariffa's head on four loaves of bread and a lump of salt. Her face, hands, arms, and feet were sprinkled thrice with water, then again her entire body, seven times. Once this ritual of purification was completed the women wrapped the body in three shrouds of white linen and three yellow silk ones, yellow being the color of heaven.

A hush settled on the gathering when the women announced that Zariffa was ready to leave the house. We followed Mansour and his family into the room. He placed Zariffa in her coffin, then his mother covered her with her crimson shawl and hammered the young woman's earrings and necklace to the headboard of the casket. When someone gave the signal, a calf was slaughtered outside the door. As Abdel Latif and Mansour stepped over the pool of blood everyone proclaimed "There is no God but Allah, and Muhammad is His Prophet—*La il Allah, Muhammadu Rasool Allah!*" As a gesture of grief, the women powdered their heads with dust and continued to wail.

The mourners circled the village three times, the village that had witnessed Zariffa's games, her songs, and her suffering. Stopping at the holy man's mausoleum, the bearers set down the casket and prayed before delivering the young woman to her final resting place.

The village cemetery was just beyond the cultivated land, on the edge of the desert. A shallow grave had been dug to avoid the body floating away when the Nile flooded and the water table rose. Zariffa's body was removed from the casket as Muslim ritual required. The mourners prayed again. The grave digger, too, did his part, whispering his last recommendations into Zariffa's ear before lowering her into the ground.

The men went back to work and the women returned to Mansour's house. The men left their fields early, keeping vigil in the funerary tent. A sheikh had been hired to chant the Quran. Neighbors sent trays of food—boiled meat and rice . . . The men ate, drank coffee, and talked quietly while the women fasted, as was the custom. Some had spirited away a hard-boiled egg, a dry cake and secretly nibbled . . . Suddenly there was an uproar. Zariffa's mother had surprised Mansour's mother with her mouth full: "Eating! Have you no respect for the dead, you heartless wench! Oh, if only we had waited for Ahmad Abdou!" Mansour's mother lashed back, "Don't you dare utter that madman's name in my presence!" They would have come to blows, had others not intervened. Once the mothers had returned to their senses, the lamenting took up again and continued all night.

13 ▪ THE LOVERS

In the middle of a cotton field, within sight of the cemetery, beneath thick foliage, Ahmad Abdou lay curled like a wounded beast. The moon had not yet risen, but the sky was full of stars. Ahmad opened his eyes and stared at the dark mass of the village and the flickering lantern lights in the funerary tent in the distance. He heard faint sounds of chanting carried on the breeze and listened intently to the steady croaking of frogs in the irrigation ditches around him.

From his hideout, earlier, Ahmad had seen the mourners winding their way to the cemetery. He knew where to find Zariffa now. Suddenly, he remembered a tale of love recited by the village storyteller. The hero had risked death climbing a silken ladder into a fierce sultan's harem to rescue his beloved. Like the brave lover, Ahmad vowed that nothing and no one would keep him from Zariffa now!

The moon was rising, shimmering upon the deserted fields and the silvery tops of the date palms. Ahmad emerged from his hiding place. A gentle breeze wafted off the desert. He felt a strange lightness in his limbs. The familiar scent of the damp fields at night filled his nostrils. His pain vaporized, lifted, as if swept away by some enchanted hand. He began running toward the cemetery. Zariffa was waiting!

When he came to the grave site, Ahmad sank to his knees, stroked the freshly mounded soil as if it were his beloved's cheek, then began to dig furiously. He was fearless now. He thought nothing of being discovered nor of the sacrilege he was committing. Although his movements were hampered by the narrow grave, he found the corpse, plunged his arms into the sandy soil, and pulled Zariffa out gently.

Ahmad uncovered Zariffa's head, unwrapped the shrouds around her body, gazed upon her ashen face in the moonlight. Zariffa opened her eyes and smiled. "Oh, beloved!" she whispered, "this is our wedding night. Nothing will ever come between us . . ." Ahmad's eyes welled with tears. He took Zariffa into his arms, stroked her beautiful hair, kissed her cold lips, and finally lay beside her. Zariffa gazed at her young husband, happy.

At dawn, the grave digger returned to find Ahmad asleep, Zariffa in his arms. Shocked and dismayed, he ran back to the village to fetch help. I went with him.

I will never forget the scene I came upon that morning: Ahmad, holding a dead Zariffa in his arms, singing softly into her ear, singing a song of love . . .

The struggle to wrench Ahmad from his beloved was pathetic!

Nazira

1 ▪ MARRIAGE

How beautiful Nazira was! Draped from head to toe in voluminous black veils, how straight and supple her body was! How graceful her movements!

Whenever she walked down the streets of her neighborhood, men's eyes followed her, lusting after her. Shopkeepers stood on their doorsteps to watch her go by, envying the man whose wife she would one day become. Adolescent boys saw her in their dreams, a fleeting vision whose virginal breasts were enticingly outlined beneath the folds of her dress. Her eyes, at once daring and languorous, teased them.

Everyone who had ever seen or known Nazira sang her praises. No one wanted to miss her singing and dancing at neighborhood weddings. Men and women alike sought her company, since she was not only beautiful but sweet.

Hagg Aly, Nazira's father, was a silk merchant who had gone bankrupt. His daughter's beauty was the only capital he had left, and he vowed to marry her only to a rich man.

When Nazira turned fifteen, her mother began to speak about her to the neighborhood matchmakers. She let it be known that her daughter would go to the highest bidder, the man who would offer the family the richest dowry. Nazira herself understood what was expected of her. The look in men's eyes left no doubt in her mind that she was an object of desire and that her family could command a high price for her from a prospective bridegroom.

Often, at home, Nazira stood behind the *mashrabiyya* window of her room, looking through the cracks. She watched young men going and coming in the street below. When a handsome, strapping lad went past, particularly one striding with confidence, his tarboosh elegantly tilted to one side, Nazira's heart raced. She raised her hands in prayer and beseeched the Prophet's grandaughter, Sayyeda Zaynab, to give her such a young man for a husband.

One morning, as Nazira polished the household's water bottles, rubbing them with sand to make them shine, three dignified women in light-colored dresses came calling. They cast furtive glances in her direction before going up the stairs where her mother waited to greet them. When the door closed behind them, Nazira crept on tiptoe to spy on the visitors. The words she overheard informed her that these were relatives of a possible bridegroom. The matchmaker had promised them a jewel, and they had come to inspect.

Through the keyhole, Nazira first observed a tall, thin woman, with an exceedingly wrinkled face and an obsequious smile, making introductions: the marriage broker. Beside her was a very pretty, plump matron who sat cross-legged, leaning against the living room's sparse collection of cushions. Her eyes, darkened with kohl, her cheeks rouged, she wore a crisp lilac dress and a black silk veil artfully draped about her head and shoulders. Half a dozen gold bracelets on each of her well-rounded arms were proof of her wealth. Nazira wondered if this pretty woman was the bridegroom's mother. The son of such a mother must be handsome, she thought. But who could the third woman in the party be? She had not yet uttered a word, although Nazira observed her shaking her head, agreeing with all that the plump woman said. Was she the bridegroom's favorite aunt? The one in charge of telling him about the prospective bride?

When Nazira saw her mother get up, she rushed back downstairs and sat innocently humming a tune as she continued to polish. Without any explanation, Sitt Zanouba instructed her to wash and dress. She carefully combed her daughter's hair, opened a strongbox from which she removed a few pieces of jewelry, and told Nazira to wear them. "Come upstairs," she then commanded.

Nazira's appearance in the living room caused a stir. At once, the female tribunal scrutinized her. Uneasy and afraid at first, she was soon reassured when she detected certain small signs of approval in the eyes of the three visitors. When the plump woman invited Nazira to sit beside her, her exaggerated gestures of affection did not fool

the young woman one bit. Nazira understood that when her arm
was pinched, her hand or ankle squeezed, it was to test for plump-
ness. When one visitor called her "Dear Little Heart" and caressed
her back, it was to see that her bones did not stick out unattractively.
When another spontaneously gave her a hug, it was to ascertain that
her breasts were firm. When the woman she took to be the groom's
mother kissed her full on the mouth, it was to verify that her breath
was sweet. Finally, when she received repeated compliments on her
hair, she was obliged to unpin her thick braids to show them off.
Someone playfully tugged at them, and the tribunal was satisfied.
Only then did the servant bring the *mangal* filled with hot coals for
the coffee ceremony. Nazira was invited to prepare it. With eyes
averted, she accomplished the task with skill and grace. Finally, when
the ladies were ready to leave, Nazira accompanied them out, mouth-
ing a few deferential phrases.

As soon as the door was closed, Sitt Zanouba instructed her daughter
to throw a pinch of salt on the coals still burning in the *mangal* to
insure that the visitors would return. But this was only a precaution,
for she overheard the plump woman whispering, "This is just what we
need," as the group departed. Her face glowed with pleasure.

Four days later, the visitors came again without warning, accompanied by a fourth, an old woman with piercing eyes. They knocked
at the door early in the morning, surprising Nazira in a rumpled
dress, her hair uncombed. The young girl blushed with embarrassment as Sitt Zanouba outdid herself in words of welcome, hoping
that her daughter's appearance had not produced a bad impression.
She also hastened to chase away two black cats circling the well in
the courtyard for fear their presence might bring bad luck. She
whispered to Nazira to run and tidy herself up and turn the kitchen
broom upside down on her way, to insure the return of the visitors.
She also slipped away briefly, lighted a whole box of matches in the
mangal, and threw some more salt on the fire.

Nazira was not pleased with her mother's shenanigans. Her dreams
of a handsome young husband had vaporized when she figured out
that the bridegroom was a man in his sixties. The plump, mature
woman she had admired was not his mother but his sister. Nazira
instantly doused the fire. But had she poured the entire Nile upon
it, she would not have stemmed the course of her destiny.

Three of the visitors returned the following day. They remained a long time, negotiating. It was finally agreed that the groom would offer a dowry of eighty pounds in gold. The deal concluded, Nazira was called in. She sulked and did not smile until her future mother-in-law offered her a red velvet box. When Nazira opened it and saw her bridegroom's first gift to her, a beautiful brooch in the shape of an egret feather, studded with pink diamonds, she was dazzled. She promptly pinned it to her dress. Admiring herself in a mirror, she thought that it was not so bad after all to be engaged to a rich man.

In the days that followed, other gifts arrived. The first of these were baskets of fruit transported on a donkey-drawn cart. The donkey, decorated with strings of bells that rang as it trotted, alerted the neighbors. Everyone rushed out to see mounds of golden grapes the size of figs, scarlet peaches the size of oranges, and green mangoes so large they had each cost four piastres being carried in baskets into Nazira's house. The bridegroom's female relatives had timed their visit to coincide with the arrival of these wonders. Nazira had never seen a mango before, let alone tasted one. All the women feasted on the fruit, sighing with pleasure. They commented on the sweet taste and smooth texture of the mangoes. Everyone agreed they were like a lover's kiss.

The next day, a huge fish arrived. It had been hand picked by the bridegroom in Suez and loaded on a donkey cart. Covering the flatbed from one end to the other, it was surrounded with pink shrimp and shiny black mussels artfully arranged to offset the fish's shimmering bronze luster. This gift drew cries of admiration from the neighbors. Praising the generosity of the bridegroom, they hastened to help cut and fry the fish. Pots and pans had to be borrowed from every house in the neighborhood for a seafood feast. To Sitt Zanouba's great pride every one of her neighbors was sent home with a portion.

The following day, Sitt Zanouba's white plates were returned loaded with candy. If this is marriage, Nazira thought, delighted as a little girl with all the gifts and celebration, then it cannot be all that frightening. She was flattered by the attention she was getting, her fifteen-year-old heart so full of excitement that she forgot about the bridegroom she had never seen. The man existed only through his gifts, candies, fruits, and the promise of a life of ease and plenty.

One September night, the marriage contract was signed. Nazira was asked by the two witnesses for her agreement, of course a mere formality. She took her sweet time answering only in order not to appear eager. When she did say "yes," her agreement was reported to the *kadi*—the judge—and thus she was betrothed to Said Abdel Latif, a rich perfume wholesaler on Tarbi'a Street. Her husband was over sixty.

2 ▪ THE YOUNG SPOUSE

Tired of doing nothing, Nazira stretched out on the divan in her boudoir, bored to tears. The clock chimed seven. Her husband would soon be home from his day at work. She knew that in his honor she should have put on a fresh dress, chosen a more cheerful outfit, worn some jewelry. . . However, she lacked the energy even to change. When she looked in the mirror a sad and tired reflection stared back.

Never had the days seemed so long to Nazira as they did since she had become a bride. Early in the morning her husband left to go to his shop. She opened her eyes just long enough to smile wanly at him. As Said Abdel Latif gave all the orders to the servants before going, Nazira had no responsibilities whatsoever. She tried on her new dresses and jewelry, dabbed on perfumes from the multitude of fancy little vials that her husband brought home for her, but soon grew tired of these activities. She could not see any point in making herself alluring, however. "Whom am I trying to please?" she wondered, mimicking the expression on her husband's wrinkled face.

Her mother was a frequent visitor. She admired the furniture covered in gold leaf, the red velvet curtains, the jewelry in Nazira's strong box, repeatedly reminding her daughter of how lucky she was. She even went so far as to admit that she envied her her leisure. When Nazira's response was less than enthusiastic, Sitt Zanouba scolded her. "You must not be ungrateful," she warned, unable to understand the reason for her daughter's dejection. She herself had long ago accepted the demands of tradition and expected Nazira to do the same.

When a childhood friend of Nazira's came to visit, she too was full of admiration for the luxuries that Nazira had. She herself had recently wed a young civil servant, and they lived modestly on his fixed income. She couldn't stop exclaiming over everything. However, Nazira felt the young woman was jealous despite her fervent congratulations. Her smile was forced, and she couldn't resist alluding to Said Abdel Latif's age. Was he really able to perform the duties of a husband? Nazira pretended not to understand.

After her friend left, Nazira buried her face in a pillow and wept with rage.

It was true that she was rich, well dressed, coddled. She was surrounded with furniture made to order from the finest mahogany, trimmed with real gold fixtures. She walked on fine oriental carpets woven in Iraq and Iran. Her armoire held more than twenty exquisite dresses and countless shawls. The dining room buffets abounded with delicacies of every sort. Her husband was ever solicitous and considerate, giving her a free hand with his money and plying her with gifts.

When Said Abdel Latif kissed her cheek, took her on his knee, or caressed her, she felt she was in a father's embrace, not a husband's. One evening she giggled at the antics of a cat jumping from a table and a blunder by the little black-eyed houseboy rushing to serve her husband. Said Abdel Latif did not get the joke. But then he was amused by the cupidity of some poor tourist he had jilted. "Imagine paying three pounds for a bottle of rose water!" he guffawed, flashing his yellowing teeth. He recounted the events of the day in his shop at great length while Nazira turned her head to hide a yawn. She thought she would die of boredom.

When Abdel Latif's friends dropped in, Nazira heard their laughter in the sitting room as she slowly undressed and got ready for bed. "They're all the age of my father," she thought as she contemplated her svelte figure in the mirror. She gazed at her taut belly, touched her firm breasts. She would never know the caresses of a young, ardent husband, nor even perhaps a baby's suckling mouth. What good was all this nice furniture, these dresses, this jewelry, these perfumes? She was nothing more than a captive, an ornament. Remembering her husband, she was overcome with disgust and pretended to be asleep when he came to bed.

One night, Abdel Latif came home early, eager to be welcomed by a fresh, young wife at the end of the day's work. Nazira made an effort to indulge him, accepting a lovely bracelet of gold filigree that he immediately clamped on her wrist. She smiled to thank him as he put his arm around her waist. When he took her gently by the shoulders with his wrinkled hands and sought her lips, she offered the old man her forehead.

That night their dinner was gloomier than usual. Abdel Latif, trying to make conversation, asked his young wife how she had spent her day. Her answers were vague. Abdel Latif sought to cheer her with stories of his perfume shop, but to no avail. Not even the legendary tale of Empress Eugenie's visit to his father's shop at the time of the inauguration of the Suez Canal elicited a reaction. He told her yet again how he was the envy of his competition because American tourists preferred his essences and perfumed oils to European products. Nazira finally smiled, but escaped to her room the minute dinner was over, pretending to be indisposed.

Said Abdel Latif finally understood that Nazira's excuses were no more than the ploys—used by countless women before her—of a wife tired of her husband's attentions. There was no doubt about the chill. Shaking his head sadly, he pondered his mistake.

How ill-advised he had been—a man his age—to take such a young woman for a wife! There was only one thing to do: treat Nazira like a beloved child, spoil and pamper her, coddle and protect her, and settle for the happiness that comes of having done all he could to make her happy. It would be absurd to attempt to play the role of a lover! As Abdel Latif was neither selfish nor a tyrant, he endeavored to win Nazira's affection through kindness and tact, hoping to be forgiven for being an old man.

As hard as he tried, Abdel Latif was not able to fool himself into thinking he could feel only fatherly affection toward Nazira. During his long, often solitary evenings, he meditated upon his plight. He was in love and his love would forever remain unrequited. When he looked upon his young wife, his heart beat more quickly and a desire to kiss and caress her young flesh tormented him. Slowly he began to waste away like a caged bird left without food or water. Yet, could he give her up?

In the silence of his spacious home, the old merchant bemoaned his terrible mistake. Raising his eyes to heaven, he questioned God: "All powerful Allah, would death not have been kinder than my darling's indifference?! Is this my punishment for thinking that love could be inspired by man? Your lesson to me for wanting a young dove to brighten my home and warm my bed? Was it so wrong to think that her song would make me young again?"

Abdel Latif thought of the story of the camel herder lost in the desert who repeatedly saw water glimmering in the distance—a spring, a well, an oasis—only to find a bitter pond. He was doomed. His thirst would never be quenched.

3 ▪ THE PERFUME MERCHANT

Said Abdel Latif loved Tarbi'a Street and the shop he inherited from his father. He spent his days there weighing essences and filling vials with perfumed oils.

During business hours the neighborhood was full of life. Merchants called out to one another, greeted passing friends and acquaintances, invited one another for tea or coffee. Small donkeys trotted back and forth, their delicate hooves ringing on the cobblestones of these ancient streets. Water sellers rhythmically played their castanets as they went from house to house, carrying full goatskins and brass drinking goblets. They stopped to quench a client's thirst with a cup and chatted with a housewife before filling the conical urns in her shaded courtyard. Some merchants ground their aromatic herbs sitting on their doorsteps, others burned incense.

For more than forty years, Abdel Latif's day had been punctuated by the call to prayer by the blind muezzin's voice, raised to heaven from the neighborhood mosque. Hearing that, the devout Abdel Latif, like most of his neighbors, went to the back of his store, spread out his prayer rug, knelt facing east, and invoked the name of Allah.

Abdel Latif's shop had windows on three sides. A multitude of bottles and vials containing precious perfumes were arranged on glass shelves according to size. It was a tiny, womb-like establishment, raised a few feet above the street. The wooden floors were covered with rugs and cushions on which customers could recline.

Abdel Latif had an excellent reputation. He served not only the ladies of the aristocracy, but also those from the royal harems. With his impeccable turban and his neatly trimmed gray beard, he inspired trust. Going back and forth between his jars measuring, mixing, and decanting, he had the air of a magician. The exquisite fragrances— some subtle, others heady—that he carefully blended for each one of these ladies was suited to her age, beauty, and particular taste.

Starting in December, foreign tourists wintering in Egypt flooded his shop. All had heard of Abdel Latif and none failed to make a sensual pilgrimage to the perfume shop. Many were young women, Americans, who called out to one another in their strident voices and demanded that their guide answer questions in minute detail. Sitting on ottomans, asking to be given little stools on which to rest their feet, they lovingly caressed the shapely perfume decanters, which—Abdel Latif thought—resembled their long legs. They greeted this solemn old man with deference, imagining him an enchanter from *The Thousand and One Nights*. They watched in wonder as he mixed his essences; then, tucking their treasures safely into their purses, they felt that each tiny vial contained all the poetry and voluptuousness of the Orient.

One evening, after a group of loud, enthusiastic tourists had left, Said Abdel Latif closed his shop, ordered a cup of coffee, and sat quietly sipping it. He was in a pensive mood. He remembered a novel he had once read, translated from the French. How very different the lives of the Europeans had seemed from his own. To their world his tiny bottles of essence migrated yearly. When dabbing a drop of amber or rose upon her fur coat would one of his customers think of her sisters in Egypt doing the same, he wondered? Would one of them perhaps imagine a young Egyptian bride delicately depositing a drop upon each eyebrow, hoping to charm the bridegroom whose face she had never seen? Abdel Latif's eyes misted. This vision of a wedding night was too painful a reminder of his own unhappy state. He shook his head, thinking of the young woman waiting for him at home. He had so desired to make her happy! Yet he knew that when he returned in the evening, he would not be met by the special smile with which a woman welcomes home the man she loves. Her every gesture would be heavy with ennui.

A visitor interrupted his melancholy musings: "*Salaam Aleykum,* Abdel Latif—may God's peace be upon you," said the man.

"*Aleykum el Salaam*—peace be upon you," responded Abdel Latif, bringing his had to his heart in traditional salutation.

The visitor, Sheikh Said Abdallah, was both a merchant and a cleric. He was a vigorous-looking man with a jovial expression and a neatly trimmed gray beard, who wore the turban and blue-tasseled fez of a sheikh. He and Abdel Latif were neighbors. Sheikh Said's shop was across the way from Abdel Latif's. A lamp in his window shone on the brass trays, long-stemmed vases, goblets, and filigreed light fixtures that he sold. They glimmered as dusk fell. He left his slippers at the door and sat cross-legged on the carpet, his legs hidden beneath his flowing robes. His gestures displayed the ease of a frequent visitor. He pulled out a string of amber prayer beads and expertly twirled them between the thumb and forefinger of his right hand. He and Said Abdel Latif were longtime friends. For years they had enjoyed meeting after work to exchange news of their day and discuss business.

On that day, Sheikh Said could not help noticing his friend's melancholy expression. He said, "Abdel Latif, how you've changed in these last few months! You used to arrive at your shop looking cheerful, pleased with how well business was going. Your eyes followed all the ladies passing, draped in their veils. Sometime you could persuade one to accept one of your special concoctions, convincing them it was the best aphrodisiac! What has happened to my carefree neighbor?"

When Abdel Latif did not respond, his friend continued: "You kept saying to me, 'You fool, what are you waiting for to take a young virgin for a wife!' Do you remember? You said over and over again, Your wife is getting old and wrinkled, Said,' and you quoted proverb after proverb trying to persuade me I needed an infusion of fresh blood in my life. Don't you recall how often you repeated, 'Young flesh makes fresh,' or 'Sweet bedfellow at night, clear head when the sun shines bright,' and again, 'The wizened oak needs new sap . . . '"

Abdel Latif shook his head and finally answered: "Allah be praised for his justice is everlasting! He has punished me for having dreamed the impossible dream, my friend. I was persuaded that my gifts and money could make a woman happy and that her happiness would rejuvenate me. But my withered face has been my enemy. My tongue has been silenced, Said, and I am unloved. My young gazelle is wasting away. My caresses disgust her, and my presence is a weight. I just don't know what to do!"

Sheikh Said chuckled, exclaiming, "You old fool! Don't you know any better? What husband has ever won a woman's heart with gifts? If you wife doesn't love you it's because she's possessed by a jealous spirit! Only a *zar* can exorcise such demons. Once she's been through one, she'll become wild about you!"

Never a great believer in such superstitious practices, Abdel Latif nevertheless allowed himself to be persuaded. Desperate, he was grasping at straws.

That very night he went to see Sitt Zanouba. Nazira's mother was enthusiastic. She had been too impoverished too long to indulge in such expensive rituals and hastened to discuss the matter with her daughter. Nazira, however, knowing full well what was ailing her, did not welcome the idea. Nonetheless, at her mother's urging, under the pressure of Sitt Zanouba's embarrassed and repeated pleas, she finally gave in. The preparations would at least distract her and add some color to her days. She thought about the pleasure of going out again, of visiting shops in the Mousky and enjoying some of the activity of which marriage had deprived her.

Abdel Latif, whose hopes had been rekindled, wanted quick results. He clung to the idea that the love he could not obtain through his own efforts would somehow land in his lap as a result of magical intercessions. His mother-in-law had to temper his impatience.

"Patience, my son-in-law, patience! Don't you know that a *zar* is no small matter? First we have to consult a *codia*—she'll serve as our intermediary to the spirit world. This world of the djinns is as vast as the djinni themselves are varied! Some are Sudanese, others Moroccan or Nubian . . . Some are sheikhs, others are noblemen. There are even slaves living together with no regard to race or station . . . We must find those that can best serve our needs. We must not offend any of them by sacrificing a calf before a camel. There is a ritual to follow, and time is needed to prepare. Be patient, my son!"

Abdel Latif acquiesced, recommending to Sitt Zanouba that she find a *codia* without delay. "I'm willing to do what it takes," he added, "as long as my wife recovers her health and good humor—one hundred guineas, if that's what is needed . . . I'm not a young man any longer and my dearest wish is to hear my Nazira's laughter and song fill the house once again. And, Sitt Zanouba, if it is Allah's wish that I should die soon, mine is to have my eyes closed by Nazira's fingers, as fresh and sweet as the sweetest butter!"

4 ▪ THE *CODIA*

The very next morning, Nazira and her mother made their way toward the City of the Dead beneath the dusty white hills of the Mokattam, near the burial grounds.

"Why do *codias* settle in these godforsaken places?" asked Nazira.

"My child, you must understand that many women cannot have a *zar* conducted in their homes, fearing their neighbors' complaints or their husbands' rebuke. Few husbands like yours would agree to such magical rituals, let alone such costly ones. Also, the police might stop a *zar* because it is usually noisy and goes on all night. The authorities pursue these poor *codias* who do no harm rather than the criminals running rampant throughout the city! Here, the *codias* are left in peace. You can be sure that the dead will not complain about their drumming or loud invocations of spirits!"

Chatting all the while, Sitt Zanouba and Nazira finally reached their destination, a decrepit old house tucked away at the far end of an alley. A low door was sandwiched between two small windows protected with bars. Sitt Zanouba explained to her daughter that the *codias* had chosen this run-down place in order to avoid being harassed for bribes by local authorities. "A policeman knowing their wealth would strip them of every penny," added Sitt Zanouba.

The women jiggled an old-fashioned latch and opened the door. At the far end of a dark corridor, narrow stairs with worn steps led to the first floor. Off the landing, to the right, was a room with a dusty stone floor and a threadbare carpet. The walls had once been whitewashed but were now splattered with the blood of all the sheep sacrificed here. The smoke of countless incense burnings had blackened the ceiling. Cushions on which visitors could rest lined the walls. In the corner, on a dilapidated divan, sat a very old woman dressed all in white. Her voice trembling, she welcomed the visitors: "Ahlan wa Sahlan, itfadalluh."

Nazira was struck by the old woman's sallow face; it looked like a landscape traversed by a multitude of ravines. Her eyes were strange too; deep set, green and lustrous. The tops of her earlobes had been pierced and decorated with large silver earrings. She wore a long, fringed veil from which gold and silver amulets hung, interspersed with red and blue beads. Her hands were long and bony, wrinkled and permanently yellowed, no doubt the result of countless henna applications over the years. Her gestures caused the many silver bracelets on her arms to jingle. On her fingers she wore an extraordinary variety of rings. These were decorated with Quranic inscriptions, beads from the Sudan, sailboats, seals, and crimson stones.

"Peace be upon you, codia," Sitt Zanouba said as she entered the room. "I am bringing my daughter to you for help, wise woman. She's been getting paler every week, wasting away before my very eyes. No doctor can find anything wrong with her. You, oh codia, have supernatural powers! What others cannot see, you understand instantly. Make my girl well again, and you'll be generously rewarded."

The old woman's face remained inscrutable. She rose with difficulty and fetched some incense nuggets, which she tossed on a fire, then went to Nazira, sitting curled up on a pillow on the floor. She placed her hand on the girl's head and whispered: "Oh, venerable spirits, if you are responsible for what ails this child, make her well again. In the name of God the merciful, respond to my plea."

Nazira sat immobile. Had she been possessed she would have either yawned or wept. She did neither. It was a sure sign that no spirit had entered her body. The only spirit she was possessed of was the one Allah in all his wisdom had given her at birth. Sitt Zanouba was distressed when Nazira did not respond. She did not want to be deprived of the entertainment that a zar would provide, particularly one paid for by the generous Abdel Latif!

She sighed, "What a calamity! What shall I say to my daughter's husband? He was counting on a zar to restore her. Must he abandon the idea of his wife being cured? Such a generous man! He would spend one hundred guineas to mollify the spirits!"

The *codia* suddenly pricked up her ears. Could these visitors be more prosperous than they looked?

"This spirit is elusive, obstinate and determined to stay hidden, but I might be able to reach him," she ventured. "Come back next week and bring your daughter's headscarf—make sure she's worn it for three days at least . . ."

Sitt Zanouba sighed with relief and promised to follow the *codia*'s orders.

Three days later, she returned alone with one of Nazira's headscarves. "What will you do now?" she asked. The *codia* leaned over conspiratorially and said: "I'll bathe to purify my body; I'll fast to prepare for dreams, eating only yogurt; I'll tie your daughter's scarf around my head before I sleep and hope the spirits will manifest . . ."

When she got home, Sitt Zanouba was too excited to sleep. Bright and early she made her way back to the City of the Dead. The *codia* looked satisfied. She welcomed her and hastened to say, "I've discovered the cause of your daughter's unrest. She's inhabited by four spirits, who appeared to me as I slept. One is a handsome Bedouin riding a magnificent white camel, wearing a white silk robe and a dagger studded with precious stones at his side. The other is a sea goddess holding a fish in one hand and a brace of ducks in the other—these are symbols of her water realm. The third is a black king from the Sudan surrounded with herds of buffalo, with chickens, turkeys, and quails. The fourth, a red sultan, was trailed by a crimson sheep who stuck to him like a faithful dog. No doubt others will manifest themselves during the Zar."

Sitt Zanouba could hardly contain herself, exclaiming with astonishment every time the *codia* named one of the spirits and described it.

Finally, she was given additional instructions. To appease the spirits, Sitt Zanouba must provide the *codia* with a white silk robe and a dagger; a sheep whose wool has been dyed with henna; a hamper full of Nile fish; ducks; chickens; turkeys; and quails . . . If she really wanted to insure success, perhaps even a calf . . . These animals would be sacrificed in an effort to make Nazira well again.

Sitt Zanouba rushed home, excited, eager to begin the preparations for the *zar*.

5 ▪ THE JEWELER

For several days Nazira and her mother combed the Mousky for provisions needed for the forthcoming *zar*. They went from shop to shop staring with wonder at displays, debating how to stretch the one hundred guineas Abdel Latif had given them. They went to other *souks*—marketplaces—comparing goods. Many things had to be purchased: colorful candles, necklaces hung with amulets, small Coptic crosses, jewelry for Nazira to wear at the ceremony.

Sitt Zanouba loved the crowded streets and alleys, the bargaining in countless small shops, the budding deference of the storekeepers who had never seen her buy much of anything. Nazira turned the preparations into a game. She was happy to be free, to once more feel others around her and to relish the admiration she noted in men's eyes. Her beauty was truly something to behold. Her almond-shaped eyes, enlarged with kohl, sparkled with fun. A sheer black veil barely shielded her pretty nose and mouth, and gave her an air of coquettish mystery. Her supple body and graceful gait drew every eye. Once again, shopkeepers turned to look as she went, while passersby could not help exclaiming, "Happy the man who possesses you, enchanting one!"

Nazira, delighted at first with the compliments, soon grew melancholy. Thinking of Abdel Latif, she sighed and thought "Oh, rue the day I was possessed by such a man. . ."

As Nazira and her mother entered the *sagha*—the gold market—her spirits lifted. They admired the glittering displays in window after window, finally deciding to enter Helmy Abdel Ghaffar's shop. Necklaces, bracelets, earrings, and rings were artfully spread out in a glass case. The shop itself was a long, narrow space, dark yet cozy and welcoming. On one side a wooden bench sat in front of a small counter on which two delicate scales were placed. Behind it was a heavy, metal safe.

The jeweler invited them to sit down. He was young and handsome, elegantly attired in a green-striped silk caftan, topped with a long, gray, gabardine overcoat. His gaze was forthright and confident. His eyes were unusually dark and lustrous, his deep voice full of dignity and warmth. He gallantly offered his clients tiny cups of coffee followed by cinnamon tea and candies.

The greedy Sitt Zanouba, delighted with Helmy's delicate attentions, chatted and gushed, thanking him profusely. The young man listened distractedly to her prattle, but his eyes never left Nazira's face. An unspoken understanding instantly sprang up between them. Nazira was fascinated. No one had ever looked at her with such quiet poise nor with such intensity. Her heart fluttered. She trembled, both frightened and pleased.

This neighborhood, which she had known all of her life, suddenly seemed suffused with some special light and warmth. Savoring every moment in the jeweler's shop, she felt as if she had been miraculously awakened from a troubled sleep. Her very soul, dormant since her wedding, quivered to life.

Dazed, Nazira only glanced at the jewelry her mother held up for her. The bracelets, charms, and pendants left her cold. What thrilled her was the glow in Helmy's eyes. Instantly she felt ashamed, and she determined to shake herself free of their spell. Standing up, she pressed her mother to leave.

"Now, what?!" Sitt Zanouba wondered, knitting her brows angrily. She was exasperated with her daughter's impulsive request to go, considering it another of her caprices. It was unthinkable not to buy one of this multitude of finely crafted marvels, weighed by the jeweler gold piece after gold piece. Sitt Zanouba made excuses. Her daughter was not herself. She had been prey to some strange whims. She had become mysteriously possessed by wicked spirits. They were preparing a *zar* to rid her of them. They hoped she would soon return to her senses . . .

Helmy smiled. Looking intently at the beautiful Nazira, he answered, smiling, "When she meets the one she needs, she'll be right as rain, mother. . ." He did not press them to make a purchase. Sitt Zanouba, preoccupied with her own thoughts, missed the significance of his remark.

Helmy sensed that this young woman causing his heart to throb would one day turn his life upside down. He did not know that Nazira was married, however. He ardently wished to see her again and was certain she and her mother would return.

When they got home, Nazira went straight to bed both to hide her agitation and to avoid the ever present look of sadness in her husband's eyes. Sitt Zanouba waited for Abdel Latif, bombarding him with her tedious chitchat as soon as he walked in the door. After a detailed report of the day, she explained that they would need more time to make their purchases. Skeptical, but eager to see his wife happy, Abdel Latif acquiesced. He even suggested that they return to the jewelry shop the following day to find the accessories necessary for the *zar*.

In the morning, the women went back to Helmy's shop. Nazira trembled with pleasure, seeing the jeweler's face. His dark eyes seemed to softly embrace her, reaching the very core of her being. She was filled with a sense of sweetness hitherto unknown. In his presence she forgot all else.

When Helmy got down on his knees, gingerly taking hold of one of Nazira's feet to fit her with ankle rings, his hands trembled. His delicate touch, his eyes raised to meet hers sent tremors through her, causing her virginal heart to beat frantically. Nazira had discovered love.

Meanwhile, devouring the Turkish delight perfumed with rose water offered by the jeweler, Sitt Zanouba noticed nothing. The young people eyed each other. The discreet pressure of Helmy's hands upon Nazira's ankles, her unspoken response were proof enough of their budding feelings for one another. Nazira desired nothing more than to spend the rest of her days in Helmy's magnetic presence. Helmy desired only to take her into his arms and lavish his love upon her. Henceforth he was her lord and master and she mistress of his heart.

At noon, the muezzin's call to prayer roused them from their reveries and alerted Sitt Zanouba that it was time to go home. Nazira frowned involuntarily, but catching herself, she tried to hide her feelings. She exclaimed, "What a nuisance to have to come back again tomorrow! If we don't settle on something soon, these preparations will take forever!"

Helmy smiled. Nazira's little lie made them instant accomplices. A delicious feeling washed over him. He was certain that nothing in the world could stand between them now.

Nazira followed her mother out, pensive. She noticed nothing of the activity on the street. She paid no heed to the donkey and camel drivers shouting, "Watch your back!" Nor was she conscious, as before, of the admiring looks they cast upon her partially veiled face. She was troubled, but happy. She had finally found a reason for living.

Nazira hardly felt time passing. Her days, previously filled with deadly monotony, were now permeated with hope. For the first time in her life she was gripped by a mad desire to open her heart to someone, to be understood, to gush with that tenderness she had so jealously withheld, to adore and be adored . . .

As soon as she got home, she retreated to her room. There, she gave vent to her dreams. They were, of course, filled with images of Helmy. Over and over again, she remembered his face, his high forehead, his burning eyes. She heard the caress in his voice, relived the touch of his hand, imagined his kiss. Closing her eyes, she envisioned the two of them secretly meeting, embracing endlessly . . . A future flooded with sunshine smiled upon her.

The very next day, Nazira rushed to the *mousky* wishing she were alone. In his shop in the *sagha*, they found Helmy waiting. He looked pale and drawn, his eyes feverish, as if he had not slept. He had discovered that Nazira was married.

Nazira felt a surge of pity, but also of pleasure. Was this not proof that he loved her as much as she loved him?

Once again Helmy helped put on one bracelet after another, a pretext to feel her tender flesh beneath his burning fingers. He savored the beauty of her shapely wrists, which looked as succulent as sugar cane, he thought. But they hardly said a word to one another, their throats parched, tense with fear and the intensity of their longing. Their eyes, however, were fully eloquent.

Finally, Sitt Zanouba began to wonder about her daughter's diffidence and the merchant's reluctance to make a sale. She prodded Nazira, urging her to make up her mind. "Does it take a lifetime to pick out a few bracelets, daughter?!" she hissed.

Nazira and Helmy realized that the time had come to part. Their hearts were in pieces.

Helmy watched Nazira walk away. When she turned the corner of his busy street and disappeared, he nearly wept. How could he have fallen in love with a married woman? What was he going to do?

He took to closing his shop early, escaping to his room, avoiding his friends. His mother, with whom he lived, watched him in distress. One day she confronted him, and he confessed.

She tried to reason with him: "Don't let your feelings get the better of you, my son . . . There are others . . . You're losing your health . . . this woman belongs to another . . . Her happiness will never be in your hands . . . Get a hold of yourself, my child, or you'll end up losing your reason like your poor uncle Helmy, your namesake . . . You are too young to remember . . . He fell in love with a pasha's daughter, and stood night after night beneath her window, hoping for a sign, anything. Sometimes, she tossed him a red carnation or smiled, and he went home and wept. What you may not know is that one day, disguised as a woman, he entered the harem. He repeated his visits to her until one day she was taken to Alexandria by her family . . . Uncle Helmy could neither eat nor sleep. That's when he took me into his confidence. Every night he went up to the terrace on top of our house and gazed and gazed at the stars, singing over and over again, 'Morning star, morning star, rush to my beloved . . . Tell her that her absence is crueler than death. . . . Tell her I'm languishing, I'm dying . . .' and he was. When he discovered that she was to be wed to a rich man in Alexandria, my brother totally lost his mind. He even went to the wedding. He was like a mother losing a child, insisting on closing the dead child's eyes herself, adding to her torment. Like a stray dog, he roamed the streets . . . When she returned to live in Cairo, he circled her house, sneaked around like a thief in the night desperately trying to get a glimpse of her . . . Nothing would stop him. . . . He was impervious to cold, wind, rain . . . He returned home burning with fever at dawn one day, after one of his mad forays, and a week later he was dead. . . ."

Helmy's eyes filled with tears. His mother added, "Helmy, my son, your uncle's death broke my heart. Do you want to break my heart too? There are so many beautiful women deserving of your love, my son. Why go after what you cannot have?!"

Helmy had listened without a word to his mother's tale and only held fast to the detail about the go-between. It had given him an idea. He would see Nazira again. He would find a way. Nothing would keep them apart, nothing!

6 ▪ THE *ZAR*

O rdinarily, once the sun sets on the quiet street where Abdel Latif and Nazira live, their house grows dark and silent. However, on the night of the *zar*—just as on other special occasions, like the return of a pilgrim from Mecca—strings of tiny colored lights were strung up around the doorway of Abdel Latif's house. They twinkled gaily while brightly colored banners fluttered before the entrance way.

As night fell, women arrived. Some carried rolls of cloth tucked under their arms, others tambourines. They were greeted by the *codia*. In one hand she held an incense burner suspended by three long chains. With a sweeping motion she swung it over the hands and feet of each of the participants. The room filled with perfumed smoke and sounds of the magical incantations with which she conjured up the spirits. The women removed their street clothing—long black dresses—to reveal immaculate white gowns matching the one worn by the *codia*. Coming and going they tossed coins into an ebony box belonging to the old *codia*.

Soon, Nazira's living room was crowded with women of all ages. Everyone strolled around a large, enamel tray loaded with candies, cucumbers, fruits, and nuts. Multicolored candles, stuck in huge brass candelabra, glimmered softly. On either side of the tray, two crystal bowls held symbolic offerings: seven small mounds of grain from different plants in one, a handful of flour in the other.

One by one, the guests paid their respects to the *codia*. She passed the incense burner above their heads, momentarily wrapping them in a cloud of blue smoke. When six tambourine players began drumming, the guests settled on couches and cushions around the room, gossiping. Some women, rumored to be possessed, began circling the laden tray, rhythmically swaying from side to side. Gradually, the drumming drowned the chatter, punctuating the monotonous chant of the *codia's* assistants: "We sing praises to our lords the spirits. We praise and celebrate each one. Praise to our lords the spirits. We praise and celebrate each one . . ."

As the chanting accelerated, conversation dwindled. The air was heavy, the din intense. Abruptly, the chanting stopped, and everyone grew more attentive. The *codia* cried out, "Mamma, prince of the spirits, we praise you!" The chorus, confirming that a spirit had manifested itself, responded enthusiastically, "Praise to our lords the spirits. We praise and celebrate each one . . ."

A childhood friend of Sitt Zanouba's rose suddenly and began to dance. With shoes in hand, she proceeded in the direction of the tray. Arms raised above her head, she swayed from side to side, then back and forth like a branch in the wind. Folding over, she swept the floor with her hands, shook her hair loose, stamped her heels, keeping rhythm with the drums. Moving her hips and torso in a circle, she spun around, moaned, her eyes closed her movements choppy. Abruptly, her face tensed, she cried out, and fell panting and trembling in a heap on the floor. The trance was broken. The music halted. The *codia* tossed a handful of coarse salt upon the woman's head, tapped her vigorously on the shoulders, pushed her gently into a chair, and swung the incense burner back and forth above her feet.

Having satisfied one spirit, she invoked another. This time it was Derbo, Mamma's deputy. When he did not respond, the drumming and chanting increased, urging him appear.

The *codia* approached Rokeyya, an incredulous young woman, elegantly clad, smiling scornfully from a corner of the room where she sat on one of the few available chairs. The *codia*, confident of her powers, shook a tambourine above Rokeyya's head. Involuntarily the young woman began to tremble, her features contorting. She clenched her fists, swung her head to the right and to the left, then abruptly kicked off her shoes. The *codia*'s hands virtually flew over the taut skin of the tambourine, egging her on. As the tempo increased, Rokeyya rose, stamped her bare feet, extended her arms as if to make an offering, and went into a trance. Her friends clapped. Rokeyya swayed from side to side, now slow, now fast. She began chanting, her movements sensuous then frantic. The drumming escalated. Finally, flushed and drenched in sweat, Rokeyya spun furiously one last time and collapsed. The *codia* filled her mouth with orange-blossom water from a small flask and showered her. Minutes later, aided by her friends, Rokeyya rose and returned to her seat in a daze.

The *codia* continued to invoke images of the spirits, describing each one. First the green-turbaned Abdel Kader appeared to her; then Zeir, king of the nomads; and finally an unnamed Coptic priest, large crosses dangling from his neck and earlobes. Next she called Sultan Rifai. He appeared to her clad in his traditional red robes, a hood with a large tassle covering his head. The woman possessed by that holy man's spirit rose automatically and began to gyrate. She waved a wand hung with silver bells, crying "Allah, Allah, Allah," and invoked God's mercy. When she collapsed an imposing matron—Ya Orabi—draped in yards of gold-embroidered crimson silk, replaced her. She wore a red fez topped with a gold tassel and decorated with a brass crescent moon, and she strutted proudly. First circling the big tray in the middle of the room, then dancing suggestively, she was moved by the spirit of a handsome fortune hunter.

Rokeyya, fully recovered now, sprang to her feet and rushed to join Ya Orabi. She nestled against the matron's ample breasts, caressed her belly, thighs, knees, legs, and feet, dancing all the while. The chanting deepened, the voices grew hoarse, the drumming frantic. The noise was deafening.

Ihsan, a friend of Nazira's, her eyes burning feverishly, bounced up. Along with the others, she began to sway back and forth, her torso taking on a life of its own. She stamped her feet, shook her head wildly, loosened her hair. Finally, dazed and dishevelled, she let out a piercing cry and fell convulsed to the ground. The candles flickered and the house shook. The atmosphere was heavy with smoke. The perfume of sandalwood permeated everything. A hush descended upon the room.

Minutes later, two servants appeared in the doorway, straining under the weight of a brass tray on which a cauldron filled to the brim with water and fish had been placed. Someone struck a gong. The room grew noisy again. Women shouted, chattered, and clapped.

The *codia's* voice rose above the clamor. Repeatedly she called Safina, goddess of the seas.

Ihsan knelt, eyes half closed, hands on the ground supporting herself. Slowly, she began to sway from side to side then lunged forward toward the cauldron. One of the musicians—seemingly drunk on her own music—simultaneously did the same. Both women flailed their arms, shifted their bodies, slithered along the floor as if swimming. The *codia* hastened to hang a mermaid pendant around each of their necks. On all fours, they plunged first their heads then their hands into the cauldron, bouncing wildly. Signaled by the *codia*, four women rushed to cover them with a huge, white sheet that instantly began to undulate with their movements, simulating waves. Their ecstasy was a terrifying spectacle. Finally, throwing off the sheet they coughed and cried, sputtered and gestured, grabbing armloads of fish, which they clasped to their bosoms. They rose moaning then fell to the floor scattering the slithering fish everywhere.

At dawn the *zar* wound down and the invocations to the spirits finally ceased. Two or three women slipped out. Others collapsed exhausted upon the cushions and slept too soundly even to hear the day's first call to prayer. It was only when the sun filled the room that they awakened, rubbed their eyes, and arose. All were sore from the evening of unbridled dancing, stamping, and chanting.

Sitt Zanouba asked Nazira why she had not danced like the others. After all the *zar* was meant for her. "How do you expect to be cured if you're so careless?" she asked, frowning at her daughter.

"No spirit took possession of me, mother. What could I do?!"

Abdel Latif, eager for news of Nazira, came to inquire after his morning prayer. "Light of my eyes, has your burden been lifted? . . ."

Nazira smiled sadly. Sitting beside her old husband, she obediently took a few sips of the cinnamon tea handed to her. She returned the glass to Abdel Latif, who drained it. Her mother exclaimed with joy. This was sure sign of harmony between the spouses.

Nazira was vexed by her mother's reaction, however. She stood up and suddenly threw off the costume of the *zar* and stamped her feet in frustration. Her eyes filled with tears.

"What's wrong, my child?" the *codia* asked anxiously.

"The *zar* has done nothing to relieve me and I'm still craving a gold ankle ring and a pearl necklace!"

"You'll have them," Abdel Latif piped up, "but first you must dance. It's not too late, my child."

The *codia* chimed in: "We still have sacrifices to make, my child. Get up and dance like your husband says, and then maybe the spirit will move you. . . ."

Two calves, a young camel, a sheep, and a gazelle were led in. Two women tugged ropes decorated with bright paper garlands. The terrified animals resisted.

The drumming began again. The remaining women made a pretense of killing the sacrificial beasts, raising make-believe knives above their heads as they danced. One, who started swaying frantically in rhythm with the ever-increasing pace of the drumbeat, jumped upon the back of the sheep and crashed to the floor.

When the butcher finally arrived, he and Abdel Latif slaughtered the animals, catching their blood in a large basin. The carcasses were carried to the kitchen, and a turkey, a rabbit, ducks, chickens, and pigeons were brought in.

Nazira finally rose. Taking a duck in her right hand and a hen in her left she began to dance, imitating the women she had seen the previous night. She handed the poultry to the *codia*, poised to slit their throats. Someone beat the gong. The *codia* raised her hand, and uttering a magic formula, killed the animals one by one. The room filled with the sickly odor of blood and a great ruckus of drums, gongs, loud chanting, and moaning.

The *codia* dipped her hand in blood and anointed Nazira's cheeks, breasts, thighs, and belly. Nazira was disgusted by these rituals. Convinced they were useless, she did not hide her displeasure, running to wash. Meanwhile, the *codia* and her retinue helped themselves to the goodies left on the table at the center of the room, filling their pockets with what they could not eat.

When Nazira returned, a traditional meal was served, during which the musicians continued to drum. Women squatted around large trays laden with food—particularly meats—placed upon a rug. Custom required Nazira to be fed by the women around her. As the target of the *zar* she could ask for anything she wanted. Food would be placed in her mouth. Also, she would be kept alone in a room for the seven days following the *zar*.

Nazira dreaded this cloistering. The days seemed like centuries. At the end of the seventh day, more poultry was sacrificed, and she was finally released from the house. It felt even more like a prison than before.

7 ▪ LOVE TIME

While Nazira was suffering the ritual of the *zar*, Helmy lived in anguish. He eagerly awaited the moment when she would again enter his shop. His impatience grew as he remembered her eyes full of wonder and longing. He was certain she loved him and was anxious to declare his own love. Although he had discovered that Nazira was married, he continued to daydream about her. Her husband was old, and she had probably never been happy with him. He, Helmy, would show her what happiness really was!

Every night after work, Helmy sat in a small coffee shop near Nazira's house hoping to get a glimpse of her, even to speak to her. Nazira was still cloistered. Helmy was already conceiving of a desperate plan to break in to see her.

One day, however, he noticed a handkerchief vendor leaving Abdel Latif's house. He called to the old woman and promptly bought a dozen handkerchiefs from her. He paid generously and easily engaged her in conversation. As she gave him information about Abdel Latif's household, he realized that she would do anything for money.

He said: "Go back to Abdel Latif's house and speak to him about his wife. After you have gained his confidence, talk him into letting his wife visit my shop without her mother. If you succeed, there's a guinea in it for you . . ."

The vendor's eyes shone. She instantly understood what was expected of her and returned to Abdel Latif's house the very next day. She had no trouble persuading the desperate old man into coaxing his wife out of the house alone to pick some new jewelry for herself. Abdel Latif was certain this would be a step to winning Nazira's affections. Nazira tried to conceal her excitement, not agreeing to go out at first. She told Abdel Latif that her mother was ill and that she could not go without her. Given her youth, would it not be improper for her to go out alone? Finally, however, she conceded, but only to please him, she said. Her old husband had never found her so attractive. How graceful, how pliant, how submissive she had become. His love for her was blind.

That very same night Nazira sent the old vendor to Helmy's shop with a message. Nazira did not want to hurt the old man, but her eagerness for happiness overwhelmed her sense of loyalty to Abdel Latif. Although she had heard many tales of the sensuousness of males, of their selfishness once they had conquered the woman they loved, she persuaded herself that Helmy was a man apart. He was not like the others. He would never deceive her. She dreamed of love's delights, of experiencing a felicity denied her.

Nazira awoke at dawn the following day trembling with anticipation. For the first time in her young life she would know the meaning of happiness.

As soon as her husband had left for his shop, Nazira began to prepare. She anointed her cheeks with perfumed oil and carefully dipped her tiny ivory liner in kohl and darkened her eyes. She wore a pale-pink dress with a V-shaped neckline, revealing just enough of her delectable breasts. In her impatience to leave, she clasped her gold necklace, skipped downstairs, and rushed to the corner to meet the old go-between. Her heart thumped hard. For the first time in her life, she was experiencing a delicious sense of expectation. The full realization of the joys ahead caused her to tremble.

Feverishly Helmy waited in his shop, hoping that no client would appear to spoil his intimate encounter with Nazira. He rehearsed different phrases to express his feelings, his boundless passion for her. He was ready to devote his life to her. But would she accept him? After all, Nazira was rich and beautiful . . . Would she accept the love of a humble jeweler? Something told Helmy that she loved him and would willingly sacrifice everything to this passion, which set her eyes aglow.

Helmy imagined Nazira's face. He listened anxiously for her footsteps, looking out every few minutes. Any of the veiled figures coming up the street could be his beloved. But as each one approached, his heart sank. Not one was graceful enough to be Nazira. He repeatedly looked at the clock on the wall. Could it have stopped? The hands seemed immobile. He checked the pendulum. It swung to and fro. There was nothing wrong with his clock. It was simply too early for Nazira's visit. He would have to wait.

Finally, he saw the go-between. She was alone. His heart sank. Had something happened to Nazira? Had she been detained? The old woman chuckled and winked at him suggestively. "Good morning, Helmy," she whispered. "Our dark-eyed beauty with the ebony braids will be here in an instant. She's just behind me. I've earned my reward." Seeing Helmy's look of relief, she added: "Like all other shopkeepers, you must have a back room reserved for special clients. Go in there and wait. I'll watch the door and get rid of intruders.

Go ahead, she won't be long now." Then, chuckling again she declared, "I bet you won't be selling much jewelry this morning!"

Just then, Nazira walked in. Helmy, transfixed, stood before her. He took her hand and pressed it gently. His eyes questioned her. Was happiness really so close at hand? Nazira trembled with emotion. Tears welled up in her eyes and ran down her cheeks. Were these tears of happiness? Or fear?

"Don't cry, Nazira," Helmy said. "I've hoped so much for this meeting. I've thought of nothing else since I first saw you. I love you, Nazira. I loved you the moment I set eyes on you. To breathe the air you breathe is my only wish. My heart is bursting with feelings I don't know how to express. Beloved Nazira, be mine, don't ever leave me."

"I understand your feelings, Helmy," answered Nazira, "and I believe you. But you must know that before the third prayer of the day, I will have to return home. You know that I have a husband. I'm putting myself in danger. This is madness!" Even while saying this, Nazira smiled tenderly at Helmy. At first reticent, she was now confident. She was certain that he loved her and was ready to adore him. All she wanted now was the chance to make him happy.

Helmy said, "Well, at least for two delicious hours my eyes will drink in your beauty. But you won't come back?"

"Alas, I won't be able to come here often," Nazira responded.

Alarmed, Helmy spoke up, "We must find other ways to meet, my beloved! You're the love of my life! I love you as no man has ever loved a woman! I'd give my life for you, Nazira! And you? Don't you want me as much as I want you? Tell me you love me! Never stop!"

"I do love you, Helmy. Nothing will destroy the faith I have placed in you. I'm sure that you're not playing with my love. My dearest wish is to see you happy beside me forever. If you only knew how dismal my life has been until your eyes taught me the meaning of love!"

The young woman told Helmy the story of her sad marriage. She described the big house where she lived, deprived of tenderness and hope. She confessed her thirst for love, the revulsion she felt for her spouse, and her feigned illness. The *zar*, which had been organized to cure her, was nothing more than an excuse to see Helmy again.

Helmy drank in Nazira's words. He gazed lovingly into her eyes, at once tender and full of fire. He stroked her hands while she finished her story, raised her tapered fingers to his lips, and kissed them.

"This will all end, Nazira. Try to forget about your unhappy past. I'll be your friend. You can always tell me your troubles. My life is nothing without you now, my love, and I'll wait for you, however long it takes!" said Helmy.

He invited Nazira to have lunch, sending out for lamb kebabs, which arrived on a fine bed of herbs, accompanied by rose petal jelly and honey cakes for dessert. Helmy pressed Nazira to eat. Delicately, he broke the honey cakes and placed morsels into Nazira's mouth with his fingers. Throughout the meal they giggled, an atmosphere of gay intimacy warming their hearts.

Helmy confessed, "Nazira, you are everything I have ever dreamed of! You're so beautiful, so sweet! I know you love me as much as I love you. Why do we have to be apart?! Curse the marriage that is keeping you from me! Curse fate for having caused me to meet you too late!"

Helmy took Nazira's face between his hands and passionately kissed her eyes. Nazira shivered with sensual delight.

Just then the old go-between rapped on the door and said, "It's time to go. Time flies when you're in love, my turtle doves, but you must be cautious." In a foxy voice she added, "It will be dangerous for Nazira to come to the store again, but trust me, I'll find another way. Nazira must be more cunning. She must show herself so agreeable to her husband that he'll agree to more outings. I'll tell him I'm taking her to visit the tombs of the Sheikhs in order to mollify the spirits. He won't object to anything that promises to help him win Nazira's love!"

Helmy sighed and said, "Yes, alas, Nazira, you have a master! We are reduced to scheming! How I hate the thought of you going home to Him! How I hate the thought of his eyes on you while I pine away without you!"

Nazira comforted him, saying, "Helmy, my beloved, have you gone mad? Do you think my husband has ever seen anything of me but a somber face?! In his presence my eyes are wells of sadness, my body a tomb. Before you I had never tasted love!"

Helmy, reassured, kissed her and placed a pink velvet box in her hands, pleading with her to accept a small remembrance of their first kiss. Nazira thanked him with her eyes. Before turning to go, Nazira gazed a long moment at this man who had transfigured her existence. Then, quickly crossing the threshold of Helmy's shop, she was lost in the crowd milling about the busy street, leaving him to pay off the go-between.

The lovers' next meeting was set for the following Sunday. Helmy would live in anticipation, his every thought filled with Nazira and plans for their future. He hardly ate or slept. He trembled with fear at the thought of losing her. She had indeed become dearer to him than his life. Her image made his heart pound. He counted the days until they would be reunited and took to humming the old love song:

> Night star, night star,
> twinkle before my beloved's window
> Moonlight, moonlight beam down upon her face
> Messengers of love
> tell her
> tell her
> my heart beats for her alone . . .

8 ▪ PASSION AND FORGETFULNESS

That Sunday, it seemed to Helmy that the sun shone with greater brilliance than usual. Street vendors hawked their wares in the neighborhood. Their cries echoed in the streets below his bedroom window, seeming to praise his beloved, calling him to her. The water carrier clanging his cymbals, the jingling of bells on horse and donkey harnesses seemed to herald a day of feasting as they went by pulling carts and carriages.

Helmy dressed with special care that morning and quickly, eagerly left for his shop. He was meeting Nazira at a mosque. Long before the appointed hour, he asked a neighbor to mind the store while he went on an errand. Every face he encountered seemed radiant with his own joy, and every passerby appeared to smile upon him. He gave generously to every beggar he encountered, particularly those stationed before the mosque. In return they wished him a long and happy life.

At the mosque, Helmy performed his ablutions in the little courtyard intended for this ritual. He washed his face, hands, and feet. He moistened his elbows and doused his head and neck with water. He felt light and happy, thinking of the caresses awaiting him. The young sheikh standing at the door of the mosque took his yellow shoes with a complicitous smile. Helmy went in. The carpets beneath his bare feet felt like heavenly clouds. He knelt.

The mosque was nearly empty. Facing Mecca, he recited the opening verses from the Quran, but he thought of Nazira. He sat back on his heels and saluted the angels to his right and left. Looking up at the luminous dome above his head, he sent prayers heavenward. Invoking God, Helmy whispered: "All powerful Allah, thou who canst transform seas into mountains and mountains into oceans, thou who canst make grief turn into happiness, hear my pleas. I am burning with desire, with a flame hotter than the fires of hell. My throat is as dry as the driest desert. My heart is bleeding. I am wounded, and only you can cure me, oh Allah. Oh, God almighty, I beseech you, remove my Nazira from the clutches of the vulture who has sunk his talons into her tender flesh. We are young, Oh, Lord. We love each other . . . All merciful and compassionate Allah, hear my prayers. Make Nazira mine!"

Helmy visited the tomb of the Prophet's granddaughter. Clinging to the wrought-iron fence surrounding it, he pressed his face against the golden crescent of Islam decorating the gate. He beseeched the saintly woman to intercede on his behalf so that his prayer may be answered. He whispered: "My love is neither a sacrilege nor an infamy, oh holy one! Isn't life an act of love? Grant me your protection, and I shall bring you an offering of two grown buffalos and a blue silk veil embroidered with gold thread. I will become your faithful servant and serve your mosque for the rest of my days . . ."

As Helmy concluded his prayer, he sensed someone gazing at his back. His heart began to race as he guessed it must be Nazira. Like a thirsty traveler lost in the desert who suddenly senses the proximity of water and shade, joy overwhelmed him. Discreetly, he approached his beloved. Their eyes met. Furtively, their hands touched, and the world was forgotten. The short time they had been apart kindled their passion. Their love had grown. They were certain that nothing could keep them apart.

In the following weeks Nazira and Helmy were content with their covert meetings at the mosque. They smiled, whispered a few words, gazed at one another, believing that the saints of Islam looked kindly upon their love and protected them. They felt blessed. Soon their passion overwhelmed them, however. They felt an imperious desire to spend more time together. Their brief exchanges at the mosque were not enough.

One warm March afternoon Helmy asked Nazira to take a carriage ride with him toward the Mokattam hills. As they approached the City of the Dead where the Khalifs were buried, the air was sweet as a drop of honey on the lips. Huddled against each other, their fingers intertwined, the lovers silently savored their happiness, wishing they could keep going forever, escaping the obstacles that stood in the way of their union. The Mokattam hills before them were turning a bluish hue in the afternoon light. On their left the Red Mountain—Al Gabal al Ahmar—seemed to spread its rough, red flesh beneath the burning embrace of the sun. Cairo seemed far away, silent. Only some hundred minarets, stretching skyward like the arms of the faithful in prayer, indicated the presence of a town below.

Slowly, the horses pulling the carriage penetrated the City of the Dead. They trotted along the deserted streets, sidewalks devoid of life. The small parks were empty of children playing. Small gray houses were inhabited only by the deceased and a scattering of squatters.

Night began to fall, adding its penumbra to the thick silence of death. Only then did Nazira think of the busy city streets, twinkling with lights, and of the husband, who would come home to find her gone. She swiftly brushed aside the thought, sinking into the sweet drunkenness that had overtaken her. In this doleful place she wished only to be loved and to die.

Helmy and Nazira descended from the carriage and began to walk. Nazira's throat felt dry. She drew closer to Helmy. He put his arm around the young woman's waist and pressed her tenderly to him. Nazira's head veil had slipped down around her shoulders and strands of her hair, freed by the wind, gently grazed Helmy's forehead.

They had reached the mosque of Sultan Barkouk. Dense, mysterious shadows played behind the grilled windows of the sanctuary. Above the arches of a wall in ruins, they watched the crescent moon and one star rising. Immobile on the peak of a minaret, looking out into the distance, a black kite spread its wings. Only the scraping sound of the horses hooves and an occasional murmur from the coachman stilling his animals disturbed the peace.

Helmy and Nazira professed their love for one another. Their whispers were punctuated with sighs. They swore that no one would ever keep them from one another. Helmy drew Nazira close to his chest. They shivered with delight as their lips finally met in what seemed like a never-ending kiss.

The very next day they found a way to meet in private and became lovers. For Nazira, it was a rebirth. The naïve child who had married Abdel Latif suddenly became an audacious woman. Her beauty—a wasted gift until she met Helmy—became radiant.

Strangely, Abdel Latif suspected nothing. He noticed that his wife was happier than before and believed that she had finally come to accept her fate or that the *zar* had worked its magic. Nazira herself had grown more considerate toward him. Love taught her dissimulation. She employed every stratagem to meet Helmy. When her mother was ill, she pretended to visit her, taking some small gift. She also pretended to spend the whole day shopping in the *mousky*, returning with a piece of jewelry every time, which she cherished because it had been a gift from her lover.

Weekly she visited the public baths, supposedly spending hours at her toilet in the vast, vaulted *hammaams* with their colored glass insets and their crimson and turquoise tiled walls. Some hallways led to the baths while others led to the street. She would slip a coin to the bath attendant and escape through a back door leading to a deserted alley.

Quivering with impatient desire, Nazira hastened to a nearby house where Helmy had rented a small apartment. Helmy was neglecting his business. Nothing was important except Nazira. She always found him waiting and instantly threw herself into his embrace. He covered her with kisses. Murmuring sweet words of love they plunged to the depth of ecstasy, consumed by passion. They enjoyed as many caresses as there were seconds in the day and would have lost all sense of time had not the clock ticking on the wall brought them back to the world.

Nazira quickly dressed and rushed back to the bathhouse, abandoning her naked body to the expert hands of the masseuse and the hot moisture of the steam room. This ritual was a continuation of the delights of lovemaking. Her eyes closed, her muscles relaxed, she lay still for a long time, her body wrapped in warm, white towelling. When a servant brought lunch, she chatted with her neighbors, sharing delectable morsels. A sweet lassitude overtook her as she listened to the quiet chatter of her fellow bathers. When the call for the fourth prayer of the day wafted from nearby mosques, she knew she must go home.

To combat the sadness settling upon her when she walked into Abdel Latif's house, she daydreamed of Helmy. She imagined the life they would share, the attentions he would heap upon her, and the shiver of pleasure she would experience when she heard him come home at night.

Her husband's return cut short her reverie. Abdel Latif noticed how relaxed his young wife's features had become, as if a sweet serenity had settled upon her. Nazira, in order to keep her secret from him, attended to his needs with greater care. However, when he tried to kiss her, she turned away. Often they had dinner without exchanging a single word. Abdel Latif questioned Nazira with his eyes. He was sad and confused. She could not bring herself to assuage his anxiety, thinking only of her lover. Her home was increasingly her prison and her husband her jailer. She avoided him as much as she could, escaping to her room to dream of Helmy and the life they would share. She spent long hours gazing at his gifts of jewelry, devising ways of making herself even more beautiful. She even went so far as to write him impassioned notes about the happiness he was bringing her.

Whenever the lovers were prevented from meeting, the old handkerchief merchant served as their messenger. Nazira searched for her as soon as Abdel Latif left for work. She and Helmy exchanged burning letters in which they expressed their undying love and eternal devotion to one another.

Helmy wrote: "Be patient, oh, my eyes, if today you cannot see Nazira! Teach yourself, my heart, to survive her absences. Oh, Nazira, your image fills my every waking hour and every dream!

"I have become like the knight riding, circling beneath his beloved's window, His horse grows weary and cannot find a drop to drink. The knight must depart without a glimpse of the adored face of his beloved . . ."

Nazira responded to his lament with words of longing.

"I swear to you upon the name of the Prophet, oh, my beloved Helmy, that my mind is filled with remembrance of your tender kisses, your love. When I fail to see you, my body grows heavy and cold. I feel so alone. My heart beats with fear and trembling. Oh, my beloved, even if there were thousands of young men pressing around me, radiant as the morning sun, my eyes would see only you, you whom I shall love forever. My heart is yours entirely. Misery beside you would still feel like a world of riches, dishonor at your side a virtue . . ."

9 ▪ TRAGEDY

As time went on Helmy grew discontented. He missed Nazira as soon as she was gone. He was painfully jealous of her home and her husband and frustrated by the nights she, of course, had to spend away from him. When he woke he wanted to be able to hold her, to share endless, happy caresses. Much as Nazira reassured him that she would never belong to another, Helmy remained anxious. His face was drawn with worry. The young woman would have sacrificed anything to insure his peace of mind, but she was powerless.

One day, Nazira announced to Helmy that she was pregnant. Her face radiated the joy she felt at this new bond between them. Helmy took her into his arms with ever more fervor, determined now to act. Nazira, although she had never loved her husband, knew him to be kind. Nonetheless, she trembled at the thought of confessing her sin to him. Above all, she feared that the repercussions would prevent her from ever again seeing Helmy. She wanted more than anything to flee with her lover.

Helmy suggested taking the go-between into their confidence and asking her for help. The old woman resorted to magic, of course. She knew a blind Sheikh who could invoke the spirits by continuously reciting verses from the Quran, Surat Yasin to be exact. These spirits—djinnis—had the power to make a husband suddenly hate his wife for no apparent reason and divorce her. Sheikh Said could be found at the mosque of Sidi Al Bayoumi, where the young couple could visit him. The go-between offered to take them herself. On the appointed day, the three of them found Sheikh Said seated cross-legged in a dark courtyard. His eyes were glazed, his great white beard tangled. He held a rosary in one hand, twirling each amber bead between his fingers, chanting. He looked the part of a saint seemingly in possession of a world of secret knowledge.

The old man quickly understood what the lovers were after. He instructed them to follow him through a jungle of small, winding streets in a dark, crowded, popular quarter of the city. Nazira was terror stricken. She raised her eyes to the top of a crackling wall that cast its ominous shadow across one narrow back alley. It was topped with ancient, crumbling gargoyles that appeared like evil serpents. She shivered. From time to time, the burning scent of dry dung patties mixed with straw reached her nose. Through narrow archways, she saw black forms huddled around small fires. Nazira was on the verge of tears.

Helmy repeatedly questioned their guide as to where he was leading them. The old sheikh, a man of few words, simply gestured for them to follow him. Finally, they reached a small, low door leading to a rickety set of wooden stairs. In the deep shadows above them, they saw the faint glow of a lantern. Nazira sank onto a low divan and looked around her at the dismal chamber. The go-between sitting beside her, was silent. She had already coached Helmy on what needed to be said: "Oh, venerable Sheikh, your reputation has preceeded you. You are a saintly man. My sister here is oppressed by a jealous husband who hates her and beats her. Her husband has made her life a living hell. I beseech you: do what you can to insure that this man will divorce my sister and free her from her tormented existence. I will be eternally in your debt and will generously reward you if you succeed."

Helmy delicately placed a purse bursting with coins beside the old man. The sheikh smiled discreetly and quietly assured him that his desires would be met. He explained that he would retreat to a darkened room for forty days and nights to meditate. He would burn incense in that tightly shuttered room and recite Surat Yasin while fingering his rosary. On the last day, at midnight, he would invoke the spirits. If the cause he was pleading was a just one, they would manifest themselves and grant him his wishes.

Days, weeks passed. Surat Yasin appeared to have no effect on Abdel Latif. Nazira felt the pangs of pregnancy. She suffered sudden pallor and was racked with migraine headaches. Abdel Latif grew apprehensive. Suspecting nothing, however, he became even more attentive toward his young wife. His tender concern was a burden to her. She longed to scream the truth. Helmy persuaded her to wait. She, however, wanted only to flee to some distant village, live in peace with her beloved. Helmy explained that he must settle his business and save some money.

Finally, in a last surge of hope, Nazira and Helmy went to visit Sheikh Said again. "My children," said the old man, "I'm afraid your affair is very complex. I'm afraid of what the future holds for you. I had a vision of an old man holding a dove. I saw myself wrestling with him, trying in vain to wrench the dove away from his hands, when a vulture swooped down upon the dove, digging its talons into the bird's neck. The dove died instantly and dropped to the ground. The old man threw himself upon the lifeless body, laughing hysterically . . . I've yet to discover the meaning of this strange vision. Only Sheikh Mahmoud in Giza can interpret such riddles. You must go see him . . ."

Nazira and Helmy, apprehensive, looked at one another. They felt as if they had just been dealt a sentence of death. The next day, they went to see Sheikh Mahmoud, throwing caution to the wind. Nazira now openly braved the gossip of her neighbors and the suspicions of her husband. She and Helmy wanted to be done with the sordid situation in which they were embroiled. Nazira's belly began to swell. With every heartbeat of the little being growing within her, her anxiety increased. She was filled with dread.

In a far corner of Giza, at the end of a dusty alley, they found the house of the old magician recommended to them by Sheikh Said. He sat on a pile of cushions, surrounded by four earthen water bottles on a large tray. Helmy greeted him with respect: "We have come to seek your help in a grave matter. It concerns a woman's honor. We must safeguard it without delay."

The old man shook his head: "I don't need any further explanation; I'm a mind reader. Write down your wishes on this piece of paper; put them in this envelope and seal it; when the water bottles begin to quiver, put your ears to the tray and do what the voices you hear command."

Helmy, his eyes heavy with apprehension, could hardly believe that such a strange ritual might help them. Nonetheless he drew close to Nazira, whispered a few loving words in her ear, and wrote: "Will Nazira be able to free herself of her husband and marry the man she loves?"

He showed the paper to Nazira who gave him a weary smile and took the envelope, holding it above her head for a few minutes. Finally, the waterbottles began to shake. Helmy put his ear to the tray and heard an ominous voice saying: "Open the envelope." His heart beat with trepidation. Nazira, pale and tired, put her head on her lover's shoulder. How far away their first, happy encounter seemed! How far away the days when she had been radiant with joy and everything had appeared so easy!

Helmy removed the paper from the envelope. An answer had replaced the question he had written: "This wish cannot be fulfilled. You will suffer greatly. A crime may be involved."

Helmy blanched. Nazira sobbed: "I'm lost!"

The old sheikh, alarmed, quickly replied with words of comfort and advice: "Don't lose heart. . . . Patience is the key to deliverance . . . I'll prepare a talisman . . . Take this cockroach and sew it into the mattress on which your husband sleeps . . . Take this blade, my daughter . . . Toss it under the stairs at home . . . It'll cut your husband's desire for you . . . Take these tablets . . . Toss one on the fire each day for the coming ten days and call the king of the spirits to come to your aid . . . Say, 'Oh, King of the Djinnis, make it so Abdel Latif will look upon me with loathing! Oh, king of the Djinnis, let him detest me so that his eyes will perceive me as ugly and repulsive! Oh, King of the Djinnis, if he touches me let him draw back as if my body were a thorny acacia and let every word I utter fill his heart with bitterness! Oh, King of the Djinnis make of his hatred a bridge to my deliverance!'

Nazira did just as she was told. She pretended to be suffering from a migraine headache, which she explained to Abdel Latif was why she was so pale. She stayed home. She waited for a transformation. Nothing happened.

One morning, the old go-between announced, "I've found a woman whose body is inhabited by the spirit of a Coptic priest. Her name is Saf Saf. I believe she's what you need."

A few days later, after Abdel Latif had left for work, the old woman returned with Saf Saf. The Copt was corpulent, heavily draped in black veils, and wore a black cross around her neck. Nazira invited her up to her room, away from the prying eyes of the house servants. Instantly, Saf Saf tossed lumps of gum arabic on the burning coals in a *mangal*. Watching them twist and warp, her expression changed. Her features became contorted as she watched the lumps in the flame. Getting down on her knees before the fire she repeated in a voice full of inuendo: "A child lives in your belly, a child who will never see the light of day . . . Divorce is impossible. Your life is in danger . . . I will do everything in my power to save you . . . Wait for me at midnight . . . I'll be back . . . I'll bring ashes from the dead, water from the public baths . . . Have two loaves of bread ready when I return, also sugar, pins, a live rabbit and a fish . . . Do just as I tell you and do not weep, my child . . ."

Nazira was terror stricken. As soon as she could, she ran to tell Helmy what the old woman had predicted. She wailed, "Helmy, my Helmy, save me! Let's leave here today! Let's go far, far away! If we don't go now I will die!"

Helmy took Nazira in his arms, trying to quiet her anxious heart. He caressed her forehead tenderly and covered her cheeks with kisses. He assured her that he would protect her and that he desired only to marry her as soon as Abdel Latif agreed to a divorce. He knew that a long happy life lay ahead for them. Nazira, calmed, finally smiled and put her arms around him. For a long moment they hugged one another, but their embrace lacked the abandon of their first encounters. Cruel foreboding gripped at the hearts of the troubled lovers.

When Nazira finally took her leave, she thought she sensed a man lurking inside a doorway. She shuddered, pulled her veil snugly over her face and quickened her pace. Her husband was home when she arrived. She told him that she had been visiting a sick friend, that the women's chatter at her bedside had tired her, and that she needed to rest. She made an effort to be more gracious than usual. Abdel Latif looked at her with uneasy suspicion. After another silent meal, he was the first to retire.

Nazira shivered, waiting anxiously for midnight. She felt her courage failing, overwhelmed with a premonition that her destiny would be decided this very night.

At the appointed hour, someone scratched at her door. She listened, then tiptoed to open the door. Without a word, Saf Saf entered, threw off her clothes and began to run barefoot from one end of the room to the other, continuously striking her body with an old slipper. Intermittently, she threw a lump of sugar in some dark corner, repeating, "May all that is sweet in Nazira no longer be visible to Abdel Latif . . . Just as the sugar I have thrown here cannot be seen, may all that is sweet in Nazira no longer be visible to Abdel Latif . . ."

For several hours she frantically tossed pins in every corner of the room, trampled clothing with her feet, lacerated curtains with a blade, chanting wildly under her breath. At dawn Nazira, exhausted, had dozed off. Finally, she slit the rabbit's throat, muffling its pathetic squeals with a pillow. Severing the head, she stuffed a fistful of pins, a piece of one of Abdel Latif's shirts, and a round stone inside the body cavity and set it down in a box. Only then did she turn to Nazira. Shaking her awake, she ordered her to toss the box down a water well, a ritual intended to harden her husband's heart and cause him to divorce her.

Then she slit open the fish, and placed small pottery shards, a cockroach, a few monkey hairs, and a dead dog's tooth in its belly. She swiftly wrapped the fish in one of Abdel Latif's discarded turbans, instructing Nazira to bury it near her husband's family plot in the cemetery.

Daylight streamed through the windows when Nazira finally accompanied the sorceress to the door and watched her go down the street. She was weary and distraught. The blood rushed to her head. She had been paralyzed with fear lest Abdel Latif waken and discover the secret ceremonies. She was desperate to be delivered from the nightmare that had become her life. As she returned to her room, she was suddenly immobilized by yelling on the street. The sorceress had been seized and was being beaten. All the terrified Nazira could think of was to flee the house and find Helmy. When she was only a few steps from the door, however, two men grabbed her and shoved her back inside.

Nazira instantly knew that her dreams were shattered. She gave up without a struggle. Once the proud daughter of a respectable family, admired for her beauty, she had become an unfaithful wife. Neighbors would point accusing fingers. Ruffians were justified in persecuting her. Teetering on the verge of madness, she recognized the bullies: her father and his brother. She remained silent, however. Remorse and insult were far from her mind. She feared above all her husband's rebuke and his pain.

Grabbing her wrists and twisting them, her uncle shouted: "So it's true, Nazira! You have dishonored your family! I hadn't believed the rumors . . . What were you doing in Giza? What was that odious sorceress concocting? Why were you back in the jeweler's shop yesterday?"

Nazira bit her lip, trying not to cry. Her father yelled, "My own flesh and blood has betrayed me! You have disgraced yourself, dragged your family through stinking mud! What infamy! I wish I had never lived to see this dark day!"

The young woman was pale as death. She neither spoke nor sobbed but stood rigid. Shocked and riddled with guilt, she stared fixedly at the two men condemning her. How could she explain how miserable her life was? How could she justify the stolen hours of happiness and hope, the solace Helmy had provided? She felt the life within her stir, her child kicking, its heartbeat. She was ready to die and take it with her, but she felt she must see Helmy one last time.

Invectives rained upon her. As her father pushed her back into her rooms, Nazira became outraged at her father's curses of Helmy. Her voice returned, and her courage came back. In a desperate cry she yelled back, "I love Helmy and I always will! I'm carrying Helmy's child, and nothing in the world will wrench me away from him! I don't want this old man you've sold me to! It's your fault that I've been dishonored! Abdel Latif will know everything! I don't care what he does! I've never loved him! He disgusts me! I'll never go back to him! I want Helmy! I want to go far away from here! I want the man I love! I want to give him our child, the fruit of our love!"

Nazira broke into sobs. Her father, enraged, shouted, "You monster! You blasphemer! You unworthy slut! You'll do as I say, or I'll kill you with my own two hands! You'll never see that vile jeweler again! So much for *zars*! Rue the day that you were allowed out! I'll see to it myself that you never leave this room alone! You'll stay here from now on, under lock and key!

Nazira cried out: "You may be my father, and you may heap insults upon me, but I'm not afraid of you! Helmy will save me! You sold me to an old man I couldn't love! I'm telling you I don't belong to him any more than I belong to you! I hate you! I spit upon your faces! You'll never hold me back! I want my Helmy! Helmy, Helmy, save me!"

As the blows rained down on Nazira, she squirmed and stamped her feet, trying to get away. The servants, terrified, had fled. Nazira finally broke loose from her father's grip and bolted. Her uncle grabbed a knife and went for her, barring the door. Furious, she attacked him. The struggle was brief and violent. Nazira screamed; the sound was inhuman. She stumbled, mortally wounded. Pressing her bloodied hands against her belly, she fell to the ground, moaning. The murderer fled.

The servants rushed back, crowding around Nazira. One who had served her with passionate devotion wailed, invoking God's mercy. Another tried to stop the blood gushing from the horrible wound in her belly. Nazira's father, pale and trembling, fell against a wall and whispered, "Fetch Nazira's mother . . ." At that moment Abdel Latif walked in. Standing on the threshold, he looked around at the chaos, unbelievingly. Those in the room, their faces transformed, stared beseechingly at him without a word. He ran to Nazira, from whose mouth a sinister rattle emerged. He fell to his knees beside the young woman, covered her face with kisses, caressed her dishevelled head, and collapsed sobbing.

"Nazira, my dove, answer me! Speak to me! I'll do anything you want! You can leave if that's what you want! Just don't die! I've already forgiven you, my dove! Speak to me! It's Abdel Latif. Don't you know me? Speak to me, Nazira! I'll give you all the jewels of Cairo if you just come back! Don't die, Nazira, don't die! . . ."

Nazira's body shook in a single spasm. A hoarse rattle escaped her lips. Everyone watched in silence as the pathetic old man wrung his hands and wept.

Finally, Abdel Latif took his young wife in his arms. He put his face close to her mouth, listened desperately for a breath, but Nazira was dead. Tears streaming from his eyes, he closed hers just as the doctor and the police walked in.

The police officer questioned the father who, in a state of shock, could only repeat, "It had to be done . . . It had to be done . . . The family's honor . . . It had to be done!"

Abdel Latif, stunned, began to pray, curled up beside Nazira. When he finally rose, his breathing was even, his expression solemn. A strange sweetness had come over his old features. He wept no more, but contemplated the body with extraordinary concentration. He gazed upon Nazira's face. In death she became serene in a way he had never known her to be in life.

Finally, women streamed in to wash the body and wrap it in a shroud. Abdel Latif unlocked a massive armoire and took out flask after flask of his most precious perfumes—amber, narcissus, jasmine, mimosa, rose, heliotrope . . . One by one he poured their contents upon Nazira's body, Nazira's face, which he had so hopelessly adored.

10 ▪ THE NILE

The next morning Helmy opened his shop feeling more light-hearted than the previous night. He was determined to wrench Nazira away from her husband. He would hide her away in a village in the Delta where he had some family. He had no doubt that the indignant Abdel Latif would ultimately divorce his unfaithful wife. Nazira would be his, and they would live happily ever after.

That same night Muslims began celebrating the eve of the great feast, the Kourban Bairam. Crowds of people milled about the *mousky* in a festive mood, showing off their new clothing, window shopping, coming into Helmy's establishment to choose a piece of jewelry or just to compare prices. Helmy was full of good will. He joked with the women, put up with their sharp bargaining with good humor, and even sold them an occasional charm.

One woman wanted to sell her gold jewelry in order to buy a sheep for slaughter on the occasion of the feast. Helmy weighed them carefully and paid her generously, tossing the coins on the marble counter where they rang brightly.

A timid young man arrived to buy a bracelet for his beloved, to seal their engagement. Helmy helped him with pleasure, thinking of his own Nazira.

At noon, the jeweler said his prayers with more fervor than usual. Nazira was constantly in his thoughts. He was to see her that very afternoon. He had put behind him his anguish of the previous night, persuaded that Allah could not destroy the happiness he had already provided. He reassured himself by repeating the Prophet's words: "We have committed no sin. Allah created woman beautiful to charm and fill man's life . . ."

Helmy came early to the appointed rendezvous. His heart sang as he waited for Nazira to arrive. He felt her presence in every corner of the room. He saw her face in the mirror where she had sometimes contemplated her beauty. He imagined her feet in the little pink slippers peeking out beneath the bed. As he looked at the gold powder box he had given her, he saw Nazira in his mind's eye. After lovemaking, she had pressed her happy face against the pillows and smiled.

Helmy relived every happy moment he had spent with his beloved. The afternoon sped by. Night came and Nazira did not appear. Helmy began to worry. Was she ill? He remembered how pallid she had looked yesterday, how weary. Maybe she had confessed to her husband and been beaten and locked up. Helmy, impatient, went out to the street, looking intently at all the women passing. None was his Nazira. He went into a noisy coffeehouse where a performer was singing:

> If you want a woman's love to last
> make yourself scarce;
> absence makes the heart
> grow fonder and
> abstinence adds fuel
> to passion's fire. . . .

Helmy was disgusted. He muttered, "That may be true of other women . . . My Nazira's guileless, honest, and true. I'll devote my whole life to her. . . ."

Very late, Helmy went home, anguished. He barely slept. At dawn, he went in search of the go-between, but the old handkerchief merchant had disappeared. He would risk going directly to Nazira's house, find some way of getting a message to her. The doors were locked, the windows all tightly shuttered, but he heard whispers and sobs. He desperately queried a servant coming back from an errand: "Nazira? May you live long, my brother!" Nazira, dead! Helmy collapsed in shock, grabbing at the wall beside him convulsively. The servant rushed to his aid, and Helmy regained enough composure to question him. When he learned that Nazira had been killed his eyes glazed over. Lurching forward, without a tear or a sound, Helmy wandered off in a trance.

Helmy began to run once he reached the end of Nazira's street, bursting into the police station nearby. The tragic news was confirmed. He was told the body had been transferred to the Kasr al Aini hospital. He hailed a passing carriage, ordering the driver to rush. At the hospital gates he pleaded with the porter and the nursing staff to let him in. He was refused entrance.

In despair, Helmy walked aimlessly until he reached a street running along the river bank. His body burned with fever, and a terrible buzzing filled his head. His chest ached. He stumbled to the outskirts of the city. The houses grew sparse, and the white form of a convent perched on the river's edge appeared in the distance. Cars rushed past him on their way to Helwan. The Nile flowed slowly and ponderously beneath the crushing midday sun.

Helmy left the road. The river called to him. The mud along the banks caked his shoes as he walked across the marshy field. The reeds were thick and high around him, some crackling underfoot. Birds, alarmed, fled to the opposite shore as he approached. Their calls sounded like laments. Exhausted, Helmy lay down on a muddy hillock. He fell instantly asleep and slept fitfully, dreaming and shivering. He awoke with a start as the shadows around him deepened. The tragic news, forgotten for an instant, loomed ever more sharply before him. He got up and began to walk again.

As the sun set, blood red behind the palm trees, a quickly fading dusk gave way to nightfall. In this sad, lonely marshland, Helmy heard frogs strike up a nocturnal song. Wading, water reached his knees. Looking up, he saw the stars glittering. Not a single tear fell from his eyes. He veered off. To his left, beyond the marsh, the land rose to meet the road. From time to time headlights glimmered and faded. On his right the deep, mysterious murmur of the Nile called to him. The water rose to his thighs, reached his belly. He shivered. The moon formed a silver swatch before him, gathering up the flowing current in its luminous wake. Like some magical cloth, it settled upon the Nile, midstream.

Helmy, lured by the soft, cool light, reached for the moon.

The next morning, guards patrolling found his body. It had floated downstream and lay bobbing, lodged between one of the massive buttresses of the Kasr el Nil bridge and a black boulder beneath the river bank.

Zaheira

1 ▪ MAZGHOUNA

Roustoum Pasha's huge country house in Mazghouna overlooked the canal and was surrounded by resplendent greenery and immense fields of sugar cane. In the great hall, on the first floor, Zaheira was busy making preparations and setting a table for the masters. Roustoum Pasha and his family were expected from Cairo that night. Zaheira's grandfather, Selim, had been overseer of the family's vast agricultural estate for years. Zaheira had been raised both in the village and in the pasha's Mazghouna mansion after she had lost both parents.

Sitting beside the French doors that opened onto the spacious veranda, Selim watched his granddaughter affectionately. She hummed to herself as she worked, her bare feet lightly skimming the tiled floors as she dashed between the small kitchen and the dining room. He noted that she was growing into a graceful and willowy young woman. Two long braids of dark hair peeped out beneath the blue, beaded kerchief she always wore snugly tied about her head in peasant fashion, knotted in front. Her twinkling eyes were jet black, her skin as soft and velvety as the skin of a peach. Her lips were like the petals of a rosebud.

"There, now!" Zaheira exclaimed, "I'll fold the napkins like turbans, just like Gazbiyya taught me!"

"How pretty the table looks, Zaheira! You've learned to keep house like a lady! Happy the man whose wife you'll one day become!" declared Selim, proudly.

Zaheira giggled. "But I'll never get married, grandfather! Why would I want to leave you? Why would you want to give me away to a stranger?"

Arranging the chairs around the table, she hummed and counted: "This chair is for the pasha. This one is for my lady. This chair is for Elhamy Bey and that one for Fathiyya. And this chair is for my darling sister Gazbiyya!"

Selim, a widower for more years than he could remember, chuckled then resumed his peaceful reverie. Having faithfully served the pasha and the pasha's father before him for the better part of his life, he had finally retired and was treated like a member of the wealthy family to whom he continued to be devoted. Zaheira, his only granddaughter, was his treasure, light of his eyes and joy of his waning years. She and Gazbiyya, the pasha's youngest daughter, were born a few days apart. When Gazbiyya's mother took ill shortly after delivering, the baby girl was nursed along with Zaheira by Zaheira's mother. This practice, quite common both in the city and the country, made the girls milk sisters. This bond conferred special privileges, particularly upon the little peasant girl, Zaheira. She and Gazbiyya grew up side by side, playing together, as devoted one to the other as if they had been related by blood.

A cool, soft breeze swept the garden. It was spring. As dusk settled upon the peaceful countryside Selim gazed serenely at the familiar landscape. The palm groves in back of the mansion were already steeped in shadow. The chimneys of the sugar refineries of Hawamdiyya, still for the night, seemed less unsightly now than under the bright midday sun. Light shimmered briefly on the placid surface of the canal. In the distance, an irrigation pump hummed patiently. Beyond the cultivated lands, suspended over the narrow sliver of desert visible from the veranda, a few clouds lingered, brushed pink by the setting sun. Two pyramids were silhouetted against the sky, the soaring lines of the first sharp as steel blades. The second, more rounded above a curling base, reminded Selim of a giant paw retreating from burning sand. The vista reflected calm, but also reminded the old man of death.

Selim had been a boy when Korshed Pasha—Roustoum Pasha's father—brought him to Mazghouna. At the time, the Turks and Europeans controlled the land of Egypt. Selim's father had worked cultivating the land of a rich foreign master when uprisings in the area took place. It was said that General Orabi Pasha would rid Egypt of these intruders. Hopeful nationalists gave him their support. Selim remembered running alongside Orabi Pasha's fierce-looking soldiers, witnessing an exchange of fire during which a number of foreigners were killed. Subsequently, a handful of peasants were singled out and executed. Selim's father, a fervent patriot, was among them. Korshed Pasha was leading one of the Egyptian battalions when the young Selim, just orphaned of a father, was brought to his attention. He was touched by the boy's plight, by his forthrightness and energy, and decided to take him under his wing. He arranged to send the boy, his mother, and his sister to Mazghouna to live. The two women had cried miserably, not wanting to be uprooted, but had they remained, they would surely have starved to death. Selim was determined to leave, and they followed him.

The grateful Selim gave himself over to his master body and soul. On Korshed Pasha's estate, he climbed trees, rode every donkey in sight, and swam in the canal. As he matured, the pasha's confidence in him increased, and he was eventually appointed Superintendent of Agriculture on the estate. All his life Selim served his master loyally, watching over the family interests with vigilance.

Too old now to oversee the vast domain, Selim was content to look after the parks surrounding the mansion. He remained as loyal to Roustoum Pasha as he had been to his father, assigning the job of helping out in the house to his granddaughter, Zaheira. Roustoum Pasha was never happier than during his sojourns to the country. Selim and Zaheira looked forward to his visits. The great house, dormant when the family was in Cairo, came to life as soon as they arrived. For Zaheira, Gazbiyya's stays in particular were cause for celebration.

Selim had built a small house beyond the palm groves, not far from the pasha's mansion. He planted flowers around it and tended them with Zaheira, the only family that he had left. While she was the sunshine that warmed his old bones, and he would have happily kept her with him for the rest of his life, he was concerned about her future. He knew that she must one day marry and was anxious about the void her departure would create. Once again he turned to gaze at her. She had lighted a gas lamp and placed it in the middle of the table, but she herself was gone. He heard her voice coming from the kitchen, singing:

Whenever you grace my home,
the rooms fill with light.
The worn stones glow magically
whenever you grace my home.
Whenever you grace my home
the trees sway in celebration,
the rustle of their leaves,
sweet music to my ears.
Whenever you grace my home,
I hear the burbling of brooks,
the rush of water,
clear and sweet,
in the one thousand streams of paradise.
Whenever you grace my home,
fresh breezes . . .

Zaheira was not a little Fellaha like all the other peasant girls.
Because of her bond with Gazbiyya, she had not only shared her milk
sister's games in the country, but had gone with her to Cairo, sometimes remaining there for months. She had learned to read and write,
to play the mandolin and even consented, not without blushing, to
entertain the pasha's guests with her singing. She was treated with
respect and affection. Her grandfather, Selim, was not poor. The Fellaheen
and the servants attached to the pasha's household were touched by
Selim's quiet dignity and Zaheira's timid grace. Everyone referred to
the girl with deference as "Milk sister to the pasha's daughter."

"Happy, a thousand times happy, the man chosen by Allah to be
Zaheira's husband!" the village notables always exclaimed when they
saw her going and coming.

2 ▪ ELHAMY

A horn startled Selim from slumber. The headlights of a car
coming toward him, fleetingly illuminated the rough trunks of
the date palms on either side of the dirt road. Clouds of dust rose,
eerily white, translucent as a blanket of fog. Selim rose to meet the

masters. The car came to a halt before the wide stairs leading to the house. A tall young man emerged from a light convertible, not the pasha's limousine in which the whole family rode comfortably. He cheerfully greeted Selim, warmly pressing the old man's hands. Selim immediately recognized the pasha's eldest son, Elhamy, although he had not seen him for several years.

Elhamy had come alone, without the usual chauffeur or servants. He explained that the family was detained in Cairo because of a funeral. He himself had only recently returned from Paris, where he had been studying for eight years. He had stopped in Cairo just long enough to hug everyone, then rushed to Mazghouna. He was certain, he said, that Selim could find someone in the village to cook his meals until the household servants arrived.

"But Zaheira can cook for you, Elhamy Bey!" the old man replied promptly. "You'll see! She can bake cakes the likes of which you won't have tasted in Paris!"

Delighted, Elhamy asked, "Little Zaheira? Where is she now? She must have blossomed into a beautiful young woman, just like my sister Gazbiyya!"

Elhamy walked joyfully into the old, familiar house, accompanied by Selim who called out to his granddaughter. Zaheira emerged from the kitchen, at first confused, then recognizing the tall young man who had been her childhood playmate. She had seen him both in the country and in Cairo. They had romped in fields of brilliant alfalfa, run behind little white donkeys, and picked flowers to display in the great house. For both Zaheira and Gazbiyya, Elhamy had been the older brother, handsome as a god, hero of their childhood dreams. Zaheira had been in Cairo when he was preparing to leave for Europe. In her mind's eye she had followed him to that mysterious, unknown place called Paris. Gazbiyya had kept her up to date about Elhamy, showing her photographs of her brother dressed in European fashion, wearing a hat. Sometimes, she even heard the pasha talk about Elhamy's endless European meanders, complaining that his son was taking too long to finish his studies.

Elhamy smiled broadly, exclaiming, "How tall you've grown, little one! Heads would turn to get a glimpse of you if you lived in Cairo! All the boys in Mazghouna must be at your feet! And you, beautiful flower, is there a boy you love?"

Zaheira averted her eyes and giggled.

Elhamy teased her, "No answer? Has the cat run away with your tongue? Well, now, I'd never dare to ask you to serve me a meal, elegant young woman that you've become!"

Zaheira blushed, pleased and flattered. Instantly, she ran to the kitchen to fetch dinner, first setting down a basket of freshly baked bread and a pitcher of water before Elhamy. Her grandfather sat off to the side while the young man ate, catching him up on the state of the crops, new irrigation methods, changes among the tenant farmers and cattle raising on the estate. Elhamy listened quietly while savoring the dishes Zaheira brought out. Their perfumes contained the essence of all that he cherished in the Egyptian countryside. With robust appetite, he welcomed the delicious green Molokhiyya soup flavored with garlic, served with a dish of chopped onions in vinegar; the rice, enhanced with hot peppers and fresh tomatoes; the succulent grilled pigeons, their skins crisp and golden, and finally the honey cakes with fresh cream that Zaheira knew were his favorite dessert. He felt a surge of tenderness toward this young woman he had known all his life. What a breath of fresh air she was! How exquisite was this simple meal she had prepared! How satisfying to be home, to feel himself embraced by this eternal countryside, Egypt!

After clearing the table, Zaheira placed coffee to boil in a little brass pot on the hot coals of the *mangal*. Discreetly, she withdrew, leaving the men to serve themselves. Elhamy offered Selim a cigarette. They chatted companionably over a smoke before Selim finally took his leave, exclaiming that the entire region was ablaze with the light of the young master's return.

A lantern lighting his way, Selim walked home in a pensive mood. He found Zaheira awake. She made tea for her grandfather, and they chatted into the night, exchanging impressions and reminiscing. How much Elhamy had matured! How pleased he seemed to be back! How thrilled they were to see him after such a long absence! How wonderful his delight was at being home and at seeing them!

Zaheira, excited, talked on and on. "I remember when Elhamy Bey left for France. I don't know what it was he was going to study, maybe medicine. He visited all the sheikhs and the holy places in Cairo with the Nubian eunuch who had raised him. That old man had tears in his eyes all week!"

"What about the *hanem?*" Selim asked on cue. He had heard the story before and knew that Zaheira liked to tell it again and again.

"Elhamy Bey's mother was so sad she couldn't stop crying. The pasha told her that the experience would make their son a man they could be proud of. But she kept on crying."

"Was there a going away party?" Selim asked again.

"It was magnificent, grandfather! There were hundreds of guests who came to say good-bye, and two sheikhs chanting the Quran and reciting the story of the Prophet's birth."

"Did the reception last all night, Zaheira?" Selim asked.

"Almost all night," Zaheira said. "But, after everyone left, the *hanem* started crying again. She was sure Elhamy Bey would come home changed, his head full of all sorts of strange notions. Her cousin who was staying over tried to console her. Do you know what she said, Grandfather?"

"What?" Selim asked, smiling.

"She said, 'Do you see me lamenting and weeping, my sister? Hasn't my son been in Luxor for three years?' Elhamy Bey's mother told her that Luxor was only twenty-five stations away by train, but Paris was at least three hundred. She kept asking who would cook his meals, take care of him if he got sick . . .'"

"Mothers worry about their children even when they're grown men, Zaheira," Selim reflected.

Zaheira piped up, "But you see, the *hanem* thought he might come back a different man. She kept saying, 'Will he still like the sweets I prepare for him? Will he find us ridiculous compared with the Parisians?' It took a lot of courage to travel three hundred stations away from home, didn't it grandfather?"

Selim nodded and Zaheira exclaimed, "But, Elhamy Bey did come back just the same and he still loves Mazghouna! He hasn't put on airs . . . Did you see how he instantly recognized us despite his long absence and all the strangers he must have befriended over there!"

Finally, Selim doused the lantern and urged Zaheira to get some rest.

In his big, quiet house Elhamy too was getting ready for bed. He went happily back to his childhood room with its bare, whitewashed walls and rustic furniture. The bed of painted wood, the matching armoire and dresser, the free-standing mirror in one corner were exactly as he remembered them. With the pleasure of a man returning home, he inhaled deeply. The night air was permeated with the scent of alfalfa and Egyptian soil, the perfume of orange blossom, the distant hum of the village, the occasional yelping of a dog, the hooting of an owl.

How far away Paris seemed with its tumultuous traffic, its overcast skies, rain obstinately pounding the windows of Elhamy's tiny apartment on Rue Vaugirard, near the faculty of medicine! It was all part of another life. For a moment Elhamy was transported back, however. He thought of the Luxembourg gardens and his lazy strolls among the tulips, their heads turned toward the sun, welcoming spring. He remembered the café terraces where he sat when the weather was nice, the smoky bars where he met friends, engaged in animated conversation, the feverish crowds . . . When it was time to sail home, Elhamy had found excuses to remain in Paris another six months, absorbing the feel of the city one last winter. As he was rich, he never lacked for comforts or for company. He was known for his generosity, inviting his friends more often than he was invited. In Montparnasse, at La Coupole or Vikings he was always surrounded by a troupe of vivacious companions who had nicknamed him "Le Bel Egyptian." Young women clung to him, Parisians whose hair was bleached too blond, lips painted too red . . .

The night before the start of his journey home, he had celebrated one last time. In the wee hours of the morning his friends had accompanied him to the train station. Their goodbyes were emotional and tearful. They waved and blew kisses as the train pulled out, heading south toward Marseilles and the steamer that would carry Elhamy across the Mediterranean, to Alexandria.

As he began to doze, Elhamy revisited the faces that had only yesterday been so familiar. Now, they were part of a closed chapter in his life. He remembered the young women he had seduced with charm, sometimes with gifts. He had been proud of these conquests. A few times he had even come close to commitment, but had broken free. In his heart of hearts Elhamy was more prudent than sentimental, even a little hard. There had been sighs, tears, and occasionally words of reproach from those he had loved and left. He had always found ways to untangle himself before it was too late, writing a flowery letter of farewell, offering a sumptuous gift.

In Europe, he wanted to experience the charms of the opposite sex. Unlike the 'carefully guarded young women at home, Parisians were open to romance. He was charmed and then seduced by the novelty of tender first encounters, spirited conversation, and suggestive repartee. But, going from flower to flower, he grew bored. One young woman, however, stood out in his mind, a Romanian law student who called herself a feminist. Thadoriza had been the companion of his last few months in Paris. Her serious demeanor, languorous eyes, high cheek bones, and small, determined mouth had captivated him. She was someone who despised the momentary trysts in which her fellow students readily engaged, confessing to the handsome Egyptian that she longed for a lasting relationship. She had succumbed to his charm and he to her passion. He nearly proposed. He could still feel the delicious sting of their final kiss. When he announced that he was returning to Egypt alone, however, she pulled away, refused to accept his parting gifts or even to see him again. Elhamy knew she had truly loved him. Would she die of grief? Kill herself? No, no, that was the stuff of novels!

Brushing away his reminiscences, he began to think of the life that lay ahead. He had successfully completed his training as a medical doctor. He had matured, experienced life. It was time to settle down, learn about managing Mazghouna from his father, who was getting older, set up a medical practice, assume the responsibilities of a family man, and take his place in society. His student days were over.

Elhamy turned over, yawned, and stretched. How good it was to be in such familiar surroundings! How delectably secure he felt, lying between these crisp, white sheets still smelling of sunshine, just like when he was a boy!

Slipping gently into sleep, Elhamy was utterly at peace, more content than he had been in years. Mazghouna, the big, silent house, the eternal Egyptian countryside embraced him. He was home.

3 ▪ SPRING

E lhamy woke up to the sound of a cock crowing. He heard the pitter-patter of donkeys' hooves, and the strident voices of the Fellaheen heading for the fields, shouting to encourage their animals along. He sprang out of bed and threw open the shutters. The sun had just cleared the tops of the palm trees, flooding his room like a warm caress. The leaves of the orange and lemon trees were still shiny with dew and the palm fronds glinted silver. Kites circled above the orchard, then flew across the Nile to the white limestone hills of Helwan. A light spring breeze carried the garden perfumes up to him. He sighed.

As he dressed, Elhamy gazed at the landscape with new eyes. Stepping onto his balcony, he glimpsed a small figure darting in and out of the thick foliage, now bending, now standing, fading and reappearing a little closer. Shading his eyes he finally recognized the graceful Zaheira.

Beyond the garden, the fields were a luminous green, bathed in early morning light. The scene was so peaceful that the young man felt his heart leap with joy, rejuvenated. Fully rested after a good night's sleep, he dashed downstairs. He was eager to participate in the bucolic scene, to share his joy with Zaheira, whom his teasing had intimidated the night before. He smiled, remembering. She seemed so accepting of her place in life, so reserved, so different from the boisterous young women he had known in the Latin quarter of Paris. In the garden, he found her smiling, holding a colorful bouquet, her face framed between the delicate branches of a white climbing rose and a mimosa covered in golden blooms.

"Aren't our Egyptian flowers the prettiest?" Zaheira exclaimed after bidding Elhamy good morning.

"And how much prettier our young women!" Elhamy laughed.

Zaheira felt Elhamy's eyes on her, dark, piercing as a desert hawk's. His face, tanned and freshly shaven, glowed like the edge of a fine saber. In a gesture she remembered, Elhamy smoothed back his thick black hair using both hands. Zaheira thought she had never seen a handsomer man in her life. She blushed, her heart racing. Elhamy was shamelessly scrutinizing her. His intensity troubled her, but she regained her composure and asked politely, "Did you have a restful night? Were you awakened by the sound of the cock crowing and the shouts of our Fellaheen?"

"Thanks be to God, Zaheira, I slept better than I have in years. How wonderful to waken to birdsong and fresh air, far from car horns and squealing bus tires! I had forgotten how beautiful our countryside is! . . . And our young women!" answered Elhamy.

Zaheira averted her eyes and bolted. She shouted back, "I'll get your breakfast ready, ya Bey, make tea and heat the milk . . ."

"Oh! you naughty little girl!" exclaimed Elhamy, "The soul of a poet has sprouted, and you talk to me of tea and milk?! I'll be in shortly to savor everything you serve me with your sweet hands. First I want to visit the trees I climbed as a boy . . . Won't you come along? Guide me? Tell me the names of the plants . . . I've forgotten the footpath we took . . ."

"I wouldn't dream of it!" Zaheira cried, "Let me call Grandfather. He knows every tree and plant, every path . . ."

"But, Zaheira, you can't be afraid of Gazbiyya's big brother, can you? Don't be so shy around me, gazelle. Forget breakfast and talk to me. Do you know that it's been years since I've heard the beautiful voices of my home girls? The Parisians speak so differently, their words are like rushing torrents, sharp, like this . . ." said Elhamy, mimicking them.

Zaheira burst out laughing, cheeks still flushed but reassured and emboldened now. Elhamy's eyes took in her face, her pretty shoulders, her light-colored dress with its snug, peasant-style bodice . . . He sensed Zaheira's excitement and was pleased. He drew closer, and they walked side by side. He picked a spring flower, asked her the name of a plant, inquired about this neighbor and that one, even got Zaheira to talk about herself. He was elated. This was all so delicious!

In the days that followed, before his family joined him, Elhamy visited the fields, spoke to the Fellaheen, even went as far as the edge of the desert. He took note of the newly planted date palms irrigated by water running in small, muddy ditches, watched scarabs—those beetles deemed sacred by the ancient Egyptians—scampering along the sand, amused to see them freeze when they sensed his footsteps. The sweet spring sun enchanted Elhamy. He absorbed every part of the vibrant landscape, listened with exquisite pleasure to the sounds of his countryside, inhaled its smells, his heart brimming with contentment.

At night, tired after his wanderings, he returned home, pleased with the idea of seeing Zaheira again. His face brightened when he heard her singing in the kitchen or speaking with her grandfather on the terrace. Often, he joined them, teasing Zaheira, like a sister, in the presence of the old man. Selim, proud of his young master, treated him with deference. Elhamy complimented Zaheira and chuckled happily at her embarrassment. Sometimes, to keep her beside him, he told stories about his life in Paris, describing the boulevards, the student dances, the evenings full of talk and laughter in the cafés, the trees, the countryside surrounding the capital. He also proudly told of the more than twenty rivers he had seen, stressing that unlike the majestic Nile, none ever flooded their banks.

Zaheira, wide-eyed, listened to the strange world Elhamy described. Her eyes shone with innocent curiosity and delight. She became even more radiant than before. Elhamy, moved, found himself suddenly speechless and rose to smoke a cigarette in the garden. He was stirred by Zaheira's simple beauty and grace but had not guessed yet how completely he had captured her heart.

With nascent coquetry, Zaheira sometimes lingered in her room, putting on her prettiest dresses, pinning a silver brooch to her bodice, deeply outlining her eyes with kohl. Her long dark lashes were admired by all the young men of the village. Mornings, she tidied Elhamy's room, touched his silk pajamas, folded his suits, replaced his toiletries in the yellow leather pouch he had brought from Paris. She surreptitiously glanced at photos of young women with curly hair and extravagantly cut dresses arranged in an album beside Elhamy's bulky medical books, finally looking at her image in his mirror. Yes, she too was beautiful!

At night, as she prepared the after-dinner coffee on the *mangal*, she couldn't help staring at Elhamy. She wondered if he missed the Paris coffee houses, their lights, their mirrors, the friends, and the beautiful women who had been his companions there . . .

4 ▪ A MASTER

A few days into his visit, Elhamy received word that his family was on its way to Mazghouna. He informed Selim, who carried the news to the village. Everyone would want to celebrate the return of the beloved master.

The following morning Elhamy saw a crowd from the village gathered in the courtyard. In the front parlor, Selim conversed with the mayor of the province and his deputy. These men came to pay their respects. They owed their positions to Roustoum Pasha. As elections in the village were never contested, the villagers automatically backed the pasha's candidates. No man in the province would have dared oppose him for fear, not only of being shunned, but of losing water rights and risking ruin. The pasha's influence assured the region an abundant supply of water for agriculture, exemptions from military service for the young village men, and jobs, often in civil service in Cairo. Also, thanks to him, excellent teachers were dispatched to the village schools, and violent crimes and thefts were controlled.

The lively crowd waited impatiently for the pasha to arrive. In a festive spirit, everyone had cleaned, washed, polished their front doors and even the hooves of their donkeys. Children ran hither and thither shouting gaily, dressed in their best. Finally, a limousine pulled up, followed by two cars in which the servants rode—women in one, men in the other—along with household appliances, kitchen utensils, baskets of supplies, necessities, and luggage.

The pasha's wife and daughter descended first, going immediately into the house. The pasha was welcomed by Selim, who rushed forward to kiss his hand and escort him through the crowd of peasants lining both sides of the walk. Before the steps leading to the house, a calf was slaughtered, its blood soaking the packed dirt. The pasha crossed the puddle, recognizing this traditional gesture of respect and welcome.

The village notables followed him into the parlor with its oversized, gilded chairs and sofas. All greeted him with flowery words of welcome, kissing his hand. He responded with a few words to each and invited the mayor and his deputy to sit beside him. Finally, as a measure of his appreciation, he accepted dinner invitations first to the mayor's home, then to the deputy's. Elhamy accompanied his father, listening to discussions of provincial politics, local agriculture, the sale of cotton crops, and their export from the port city of Alexandria. After a meal of roast lamb, the pasha received the compliments and complaints of the peasants who respectfully and often obsequiously took turns speaking, standing before their master and landlord. They called him "The Just," "The Compassionate," "The Wise . . ." His visits, eagerly awaited, were the time to ask for favors, discuss grievances, or seek help in redressing some injustice.

A woman pleaded to be admitted to the first audience. She begged and cried so persuasively and loudly that the servants finally allowed her in. She knelt before the pasha, kissed his hands, her eyes shining with tears of rage. Her lips trembled as she cried, "Master, you cannot imagine the indignity I have suffered! Salhiyya threw sand in my honey and dirt in my butter! May God squash this vermin who passes for a woman!"

The pasha listened patiently and threw a warning glance at Elhamy, who was chuckling. His son must learn to respect the concerns of humble and great alike. Then, turning to the woman, whose name was Fatouma, Roustoum Pasha ordered her to stand up and explain the situation. It was a quarrel between co-wives. Fatouma and Salhiyya were married to Sheikh Massad, who lived one village over from Mazghouna. One of the pasha's most reliable tenant farmers, he was an upstanding citizen who paid his rent on time and kept his larder full. Following the death of their husband, the two wives began to fight over provisions of clarified butter, honey, fruit, and vegetable preserves . . . Fatouma, the Sheikh's first wife, grabbed the better part for herself and her children. Salhiyya secretly swore to take revenge. She set out to spoil her rival's stores, kneading dirt into her butter, feces into her preserves, and sand into her honey. Despite himself, the pasha could not restrain a smile, hearing about these pranks. Finally, he admonished both women and ordered the younger Salhiyya and her children to give a share of the goods to Fatouma and her children.

Next, Sheikh Saleh, a corpulent village notable in his sixties, stepped up, panting. He owned fifty *feddans* of fertile land, ten cows, five water buffalos, and had two wives and countless children. He would have finished his days in peace had he not suddenly been smitten with a young peasant by the name of Mabrouka, poor, but fresh as a new ear of corn picked on a summer morning.

Sheikh Saleh's first wife had been chosen for him by his father as was the custom. The second was a marriage of convenience entered into to acquire a piece of land bordering the canal, across the way from his own. Now, he decided he had earned the right to indulge himself, disregarding the objections of his wives and children. He turned a deaf ear, prepared to put up with their envy and jealousy rather than give up Mabrouka. The beauty of his young bride was worth it, he felt. He had not considered how tiring love at his

advanced age could be. Shortly after the wedding, he took ill. Everyone, even the village doctor, blamed it on the excessive demands of
his young bride. While Sheikh Saleh lay nearly dying, the family had
obtained a divorce decree, helped by a cousin who was a local judge.
Sheikh Saleh, however, was not about to be led down the primrose
path to an afterlife full of seductive *houris*! He hung onto life and
recovered. He was, of course, enraged at the trick played upon him
and quarreled with his relatives, insisting they bring Mabrouka back.
His sons declared that they would turn their backs on him if he
remarried her and his sons-in-law—egged on by their wives—swore
they would divorce his daughters if he persisted.

Perplexed and outraged, Sheikh Saleh asked the pasha to intervene. This was a delicate matter. The pasha could not outright
declare the divorce null and void for fear of undermining the
judge's authority, embarrassing Sheikh Saleh's sons, daughters, nephews, and nieces before the entire village. Roustoum Pasha took
Elhamy as a go-between. Mabrouka, who was present, guessed that
the young master would defend her. Father and son conferred, the
pasha finally ordering Sheikh Saleh's sons to return the divorced
Mabrouka's dowry to her. It consisted of three hundred pounds.
They protested. It was clear that they preferred having the young
bride returned to their father's bed to losing such a substantial sum
of money. The pasha was able to dispense justice without alienating
any of the players by declaring that upon Sheikh Saleh's death—
after a long life, of course—Mabrouka would relinquish her share
of inheritance if she married again.

Everyone congratulated Roustoum Pasha and Elhamy Bey on
their wisdom and the finesse with which they handled such a delicate situation.

For a time, Elhamy was amused by these village tussles. He
admired his father's patience with the peasants, his thoughtful media-
tion of their conflicts. But the novelty of these encounters soon wore
off, leaving room only for the tedium. He wondered how many tiny
cups of coffee he could stand to drink in the company of these
villagers, dutifully accepting their hospitality, shaking his head respectfully in response to every one of his father's pronouncements,
not daring—out of a sense of decorum—even to smoke in the
pasha's presence. He longed for the company of his mother, sister, and

the graceful Zaheira, whose laughter had filled his first happy days in Mazghouna.

5 ▪ GAZBIYYA

Gazbiyya had enthusiastically rushed into the arms of her childhood friend with cries of joy. They had not seen each other for over two years. Since Zaheira's mother's death, the young girl had not once been to the city. Gazbiyya—now a young woman of marriageable age—had a busy social schedule and accompanied her parents here and there. In winter, they went to the health station of Helwan where the pasha took the waters to relieve his rheumatisms. In spring, the family socialized in Cairo. Summers, the entire household moved to Alexandria, to their villa on the Mediterranean. Gazbiyya had missed Mazghouna and her milk sister. She and Zaheira had a lot of catching up to do!

While the servants were busy cleaning and cooking, Zaheira helped Gazbiyya unpack and hang her dresses in the old maple armoire of her childhood room. The girls chattered nonstop.

"How you've blossomed my little Zaheira!" Gazbiyya exclaimed. "How I envy you living year round in this peaceful countryside! What have you been doing these last two years? Tell me everything!"

"My life is monotonous, Gazbiyya. Nothing happens. I clean, work in the fields, water the flowers, shop and cook, particularly what Sidi likes. I keep accounts of household expenses, and in the evening I sit quietly with my grandfather on the terrace. He and I often talk about the past. Do you remember when we ran up and down the garden paths, shouting the names of flowers? Do you remember us picking figs and how we wore identical dresses? Your suitcases are full of modern outfits now, and beautiful jewelry!"

"Yes, my mother spoils me, Zaheira; she wants me to be the most beautiful young woman in all of Cairo. I'm the envy of all my friends, yet I'm less free than most. I love the life you lead, far from gossip and constant rivalries, and I often think of our childhood games. Do you remember the one where we were princesses, picking leaves and flowers and making tiaras?"

Gazbiyya sighed and put an arm around her friend. She pulled out the gifts she had brought for Zaheira and pressed her to try on some of her new outfits. Zaheira put on a flowered dress, a bracelet, a necklace . . . Gazbiyya wrapped Zaheira's braids around her head like a crown, transforming her country pal into a Parisian Miss. The girls laughed until they cried. Zaheira kept thinking about Elhamy. Would he prefer her dressed this way?

All at once Gazbiyya took on a mysterious air. She whispered, "Let me show you something while mother is downstairs ordering the servants around!"

She locked the door and got out a small, round box hidden at the bottom of her suitcase. In it was a white pillbox hat with a big black bow that she placed upon her head, rearranging her curls beneath it. This French hat, given her by a friend, made her look so impish that both girls burst out laughing. Making faces in the mirror, Zaheira exclaimed, "You look pretty, Gazbiyya, but will the pasha let you go out like this, without a veil? Don't you remember how he criticized your mother's friends for going to the theater, their faces uncovered, dressed in European fashion?"

"Oh, I didn't wear this hat out, my dear Zaheira! Only to a close friend's house this summer, and even then I added a veil . . . , a diaphanous one, though," Gazbiyya giggled.

"Do you remember when you were here last and your mother had the garden cleared of all men before going out for a walk?" asked Zaheira.

"How can I forget it?! Did you know that a lot of young women go to the university now . . . Some have dropped the veil altogether, even in the presence of men. Some of us with more conservative parents wear a thin one, like I had on when we arrived. My father doesn't like it, but he's resigned to the change. Mother's even more conservative. She'd have scolded me if she'd caught me leaving the house with this hat on . . ."

"In your place I would have been ashamed, Gazbiyya. . . . All those men, looking straight at me, even speaking to me in public . . ."

Gazbiyya was impishly delighted at being able to shock her country friend. She asked, "Do you remember our box at the opera? How it was screened in? All the ladies had to be hidden? That's all over now! Men can look at women, admire their dresses and jewelry . . ."

"Even your mother, the Sitt Hanem, sits exposed?!" Zaheira burst out.

"Oh, no, not mother! We'll be the last to give up our stuffy old cage! Father will not hear of removing the Mashrabiyya screens . . . With Elhamy here to escort us, though, maybe he'll become more lenient. Mother has allowed me to go out to the shops only this year! It's so much fun, Zaheira. I'll take you when you come to Cairo. You can browse, finger the fabrics, try on clothes, watch the men watching you without seeming to, even make fun of them! You'll see!"

"You've changed, Gazbiyya . . . And Elhamy Bey seems so modern too . . . Are you forgetting our traditions?" Zaheira whispered.

"I'm still your devoted Gazbiyya, Zaheira! Elhamy's quite the Parisian, though! He came home with cases full of books and clothes, the latest in everything . . . Don't you think he's more handsome?"

Zaheira blushed, not answering. She looked at the clock and urged Gazbiyya to put everything back in place. The girls went downstairs, Zaheira feeling smug at being taken so completely into Gazbiyya's confidence. She couldn't help feeling a notch above other girls in the village. What would it be like to be thoroughly modern?

Lunch was served in the spacious dining room. Several women from the village were visiting, some sitting cross-legged on the ground, others on chairs. Selim's granddaughter was honored to serve the traditional meal of rice and roast lamb sent by the village mayor. Gazbiyya was solicitous of Zaheira, pressing her to spend every minute she could at the mansion. The pasha, whose severe demeanor kept everyone at bay, was kind to the young woman. His wife treated Zaheira like a daughter. The *hanem* was secretly pleased to have the girls back together, thinking Zaheira a better influence on her daughter than many of Gazbiyya's city friends. Everyone complimented Zaheira on how pretty she looked, transformed by the new outfit that Gazbiyya had given her.

In the evening, the family gathered over tea. Selim looked at his granddaughter with even more pride and affection than usual. Zaheira sat listening to the pasha tell story after story of his meanders through the countryside. Gazbiyya, full of mischief, teased her brother, calling him "The Parisian" and bombarding him with questions about the beautiful ladies he had met, the plays he had seen, the places he had been . . . He indulged his sister with tales of his student days, which already seemed to belong to a far distant past.

Zaheira, listening to Elhamy, was seduced by the warmth and depth of his voice. Everything glowed in his presence. She gazed at him with wonder and admiration, hanging on his every word, yet afraid to be noticed by the giggling Gazbiyya. When Elhamy patted her on the head in a friendly gesture, or touched her hand as he did his sister's, her heart raced. When he looked at her affectionately, her entire being seemed to melt. The innocent Zaheira was overcome with feelings she had never before experienced.

6 ▪ FREEDOM

Elhamy knew that he had charmed his childhood playmate. Zaheira had put a spell on him, too. In her presence, he became playful and passionate. He found her discretion and grace irresistible. Her downcast eyes when he teased her were so different from the mocking smiles and provocative looks of the Parisian women on the boulevards and cafés of the Latin quarter.

During the day, Elhamy accompanied the pasha or the family's Coptic overseer on rounds of the estate, wishing he could be with the girls instead. He was bored with the flowery greetings, the endless exchange of ritual compliments, and the lengthy discussions over cattle and crops.

One day, Elhamy proposed that Gazbiyya and Zaheira go along. Their company, he knew, would alleviate the tedium of these inspection tours along dusty country roads. Also, he was certain that Zaheira's intuition about her fellow villagers would help him. How Gazbiyya and Zaheira would giggle at the fat mayor with his naïve, childlike eyes fixed upon him, trying to ingratiate himself with the pasha's son! How the three of them would enjoy the car ride together, passing little girls playing among cows and goats, seductively draping their torn shawls, trying to act so grown up!

Gazbiyya and Zaheira were delighted with the idea and clapped their hands excitedly like children about to be given a treat. They loved riding in Elhamy's convertible, observing the serious activities of men . . . Would the pasha give them permission to go? Being allowed to romp freely in the garden and the orchard nearest the mansion had been a concession. How they appreciated every bud, every butterfly. . . Gazbiyya, a young lady now, had less freedom than her country sister and longed to run at whim through the village like Zaheira. She remembered visiting the fields, watching the Fellaheen at work, striking up a conversation with their womenfolk when she and Zaheira were little. She loved the idea of venturing out to that mysterious realm beyond the fields, the desert. Europeans rode horses and drove cars out there . . . They raced along the bumpy roads up to the high sand dunes . . . Why couldn't she do the same?

Finally, Elhamy broached the subject with the pasha. At the breakfast table one day, he stressed the importance of exercise and fresh air. Gazbiyya would benefit from walking, maybe even riding a horse.

The pasha exclaimed, "Physical exercise! What are these new-fangled ideas, my son?! Isn't housework and walking in the garden exercise enough? What's the use of mechanical movements done to the count of one, two, three? Is your sister a girl or a soldier? Women in my day never even thought of setting foot outside the home! They were content, and I assure you they enjoyed better health than the young ladies of today. Those modern misses who spend half their day at the sporting clubs give absolutely no thought to how to live in our climate. They are forever complaining of their stomachs and their livers and starve themselves to look fashionable . . . Why ape the Europeans to the detriment of our own customs and traditions?"

Shaking his head, the pasha addressed his daughter: "You're too young to be aware of politics, Gazbiyya, but all of this mishmash is the result of the events of 1919! In the name of patriotism, women have given up all discretion. They even want to get involved in politics! And, how about those who refuse to wear the veil? Will they next go naked in the streets? I hope I never see the day when my family adopts such values!"

Stammering a little, Elhamy finally dared interrupt, "Father, you know that Gazbiyya is always discreet. Virtue can't be measured by the thickness of her veil, but my sister will wear hers to go out if she must . . ."

"Praise the Lord! I'm relieved to know that the timid dove of decorum still lives under my roof! So be it. Gazbiyya can sometimes accompany you, and Zaheira can go along too if her grandfather will let her."

And so, the young people planned one excursion after another. As the girls had never been near a horse, Elhamy decided it would be safer to have them only ride the car. At first, he drove carefully on the high banks of the canals. Sometimes, he ventured on the narrow, dusty roads bordering fields of alfalfa, terrorizing water buffalo and goats with the roar of his motor. Other times he went as far as the desert, going fast then to avoid getting stuck in the soft sand. Gazbiyya loved speed and laughed uproariously at the fear on the faces of boys on their donkeys. She teased peasant girls who thinking she was a tourist, instantly hid behind their veils. Zaheira, terrified, begged Elhamy to slow down. He delighted in tormenting her, but looked so affectionately at her once the car stopped that she smiled gently, reassured.

Every now and then Gazbiyya ran into a nearby field, picked a few fava bean pods to munch on, or cut a flower. Elhamy took advantage of her absence to squeeze Zaheira's hand. Awkwardly, she raised her eyes to meet his, a smile playing about the corners of her mouth. She experienced then a new and strange sort of happiness.

One spring afternoon, the young people braved the hot, dry winds and drove across the canal to the desert. Elhamy seemed more serious than usual. He stopped the car at the foot of a steep cliff overlooking a river bed. In the distance the Giza pyramids were silhouetted against a gray sky. Extending his hands, he helped the girls over the rocks, down into the dry *wadi*. They sat on a boulder to rest. Elhamy was unusually silent. Zaheira picked up little pebbles and threw them away, gazing pensively at him. Gazbiyya, who had prattled cheerfully on the way, also grew quiet. The hot wind swirled the sand around them, and the intense midday sun made them drowsy. Leaning on a rock, Gazbiyya fell asleep.

Elhamy looked at Zaheira, who blushed. She wanted this moment to last forever. Elhamy reached for her wrists, holding them lightly, touching her arm, stroking her elbow, then her shoulder. Zaheira quivered. He put his arm around her waist and drew her close. She did not move away. When he looked intently into Zaheira's dark eyes, she closed them and he kissed her.

7 ▪ LOVE

At dusk, they started home in silence. Zaheira was agitated. She watched the green fields fly by, the peasants and their herds returning to the village. Everything seemed at once familiar and strange. She wondered what Elhamy wanted. Was this love? A game? Could Elhamy Bey really be interested in a humble country girl like herself? Troubled, she nonetheless held fast to the feeling of his sweet, lingering kiss. What should she do if he tried to kiss her again?

Gazbiyya remarked that Elhamy and Zaheira were pensive, but she was otherwise unaware of the emotions blossoming around her. Zaheira tried to conceal her feelings, only now and then discreetly returning Elhamy's complicitous smile.

That evening the family sat quietly around the dinner table with Zaheira and Selim in attendance. The pasha and his wife were astonished at the pleasure these young people took in running around all day, oblivious to heat and dust. Gazbiyya's cheeks were rosy and Zaheira's eyes brighter than usual. When the pasha conceded that these outings seemed to have done the girls a world of good, Zaheira looked down shyly, particularly avoiding her grandfather's eyes. She was quickly learning the game of dissimulation.

In her bed that night, her windows wide open to the perfumes of the orchards and the fields, Zaheira pondered the events of the day. Did this young master really love her? Would he ever consider marrying a humble country girl? What were his intentions?

Zaheira was seventeen years old. Her experiences were by and large limited to the village. The men she met were countryfolk like herself. In some ineffable way, she felt superior to them. She had never discussed this disquieting feeling called love with any of her girlfriends. Now, she secretly cherished the new realm into which Elhamy's caresses had just initiated her. Surely these feelings were not evil! She convinced herself that had Gazbiyya known, she would have approved.

Zaheira tossed and turned all night, unsettled. She could only think of tomorrow and seeing Elhamy. She believed with all her heart that his caress was her reward for a virtuous life. Finally, she dozed off, dreaming of his embrace.

How could Zaheira have known that happiness was never more than an elusive guest? Sudden as lightning? Quickly gone, leaving the heart in shreds, the soul strewn with bitter ashes?

The following day, after having contemplated herself in the mirror, Zaheira filled the pasha's house with flowers from the garden. She took particular pleasure in adorning Elhamy's room. Supervising the work the servants were doing, she dashed outside when she heard the sound of his car. In the shadowy garage, he welcomed her with open arms. She rushed into his embrace and returned his passionate kisses.

Elhamy particularly loved surprising Zaheira in the deep doorways of the big family house, and feeling her questioning eyes calling to him, her feverish lips responding to his kisses. Her body, hot and trembling in the delectable intimacy of their embrace, inspired his burning desire. There were other, surreptitious meetings. Zaheira spoke little, but her silent plea was not lost on the worldly Elhamy. She had the look of a captive doe, wishing merely to be told what was expected of her. Her sweet submissiveness was pleasing to him. He had become inured to calculating women who hastened to rearrange their curls or reapply their lipsticks after the slightest kiss. How different Zaheira was!

In the privacy of his bedroom, Elhamy whistled and hummed. He was both moved by Zaheira's freshness and thrilled with his new conquest. Zaheira, totally without artifice, had not had to be wooed with compliments and cocktails. Elhamy basked in the glow of his seductive powers and was flattered by Zaheira's prompt response to his amorous advances. The Egyptian countryside, which he was rediscovering after years of absence, suddenly seemed enchanted in the presence of this passionate yet timid young woman who loved him. All at once he felt intensely alive. Nothing could have made his homecoming sweeter. Alone, Elhamy daydreamed. He imagined Zaheira's body among the golden dunes. He saw himself lying beside

her, undressing her on the voluptuously hot sand, marrying his burning caresses to those of the sun. However, cautious and keenly aware
of his responsibility toward this childhood playmate whom Selim had
entrusted to his family, he restrained himself. Was she expecting
marriage? He was not ready to be tied down, and besides, this was
a passing fancy that the realities of his life could not sustain. Zaheira
did not really fit in. How could she converse with the elegant ladies
he met on the beach at Alexandria? What impression would she
make on important personages—diplomats and professionals—with
whom he socialized? He could not imagine, for example, a cruise to
Europe accompanied by this graceful but naïve woman who spoke
only Arabic. Were he to marry Zaheira, she would no doubt be a
loyal spouse, but one he would have to keep hidden. What an impossible situation!

Elhamy's scruples kept him from realizing his fantasy: slipping
out at night and finding his way to Zaheira's bedroom. He was
certain, however, that had he done so she would not have resisted,
offering him her warm breasts, her virginal hips. He burned with the
memory of their last kiss but knew that if she became his, he could
not abandon her. Her family would be shamed and touted by the
whole village. His uncompromising father would oblige him to marry
her. Elhamy could not afford to jeopardize his future for a moment
of idyllic delight.

The next day he found and kissed Zaheira again, then went off
by himself into the garden. Like most men, Elhamy was selfish. He
reflected, "If women were reasonable they'd understand our caprices
and take them in stride. Desire is natural. If only they wouldn't look
so anguished whenever they're expecting a kiss! If only they'd spare
us the scenes, the punishing laments!" Elhamy could not have been
thinking of Zaheira, yet in that instant he had lumped her in with
every woman he had loved and left. He resolved to abandon all
further thought of seduction. Henceforth he would avoid Zaheira.
He was certain she would soon forget him, marry one of her kind,
and live happily ever after. Later, they might exchange a few words,
indulge in a lingering handshake, and only they would be privy to
the tenderness that had once passed between them. For Elhamy,
Zaheira was already becoming a memory.

8 ▪ MOUNIRA

Zaheira was worried. Elhamy's conspiratorial glances in her direction had disappeared. His triumphant smile was gone. He barely spoke to her. For two days—an eternity to Zaheira—he was totally occupied with his father. How had she displeased him? Sophisticated Parisian that he now was, he must be wise to the secrets of love known to married women and courtesans. Was she too inexperienced to hold his interest? A couple of times, her heart pounding, she went into Elhamy's room, to be close to his things if not to him. While he and his father talked about this and that on the veranda downstairs, Zaheira collapsed on Elhamy's bed and cried her eyes out. Reality brought her up short. How could she dream of her master's son!

The house was in an uproar. Company was expected. Zaheira caught the other servants whispering mysteriously. One morning, Elhamy and Gazbiyya were gone without a word. The pasha's wife, the *hanem*, told her that they had driven to El Ayrab to fetch guests, and that she must prepare the upstairs rooms. Fakhry Pasha, a kin of her husband and a man of considerable means, she told Zaheira, was coming to stay a few days along with his wife and daughter Mounira. He had studied in europe and had raised his daughter accordingly. The *hanem* was not sure she approved, but her husband was seriously considering Mounira as a prospective bride for Elhamy. This visit was a scheme to get the two together. Zaheira leaned on a dresser to keep from collapsing. Now she understood Elhamy's behavior. His cousin Mounira was rich and worldly. He would court her and toss aside any thought of the innocent kisses of a simple country girl. Zaheira had been too trusting. She blamed herself for forgetting her place, which was only to serve her masters. Before long she would be obliged to wait on this new stranger, even to smile. She would have to look on as Mounira sat beside Elhamy in his car . . . Mounira would return his passionate caresses . . . They would laugh together over how easily he had captured this unsuspecting bird . . . He would describe how awkwardly Zaheira had kissed him . . . She was ashamed and profoundly humiliated.

On the pretext that she was needed in the kitchen, Zaheira escaped the *hanem*'s possible scrutiny. Outside, in the garden, the scene of her budding love, she burst into tears. She could not find it in her heart to blame Elhamy, though. She had loved him but had been a fool to think that she could ever share his life. Another woman would have him, a woman whom she would have to serve. Zaheira wanted desperately to unburden her heart. But to whom? Her girlfriends would blame her. Gazbiyya, she realized now, would pity her. Her grandfather, much as he loved her, would reprimand her. Better suffer in silence, try to forget.

Zaheira rose and stole over to the fountain. Cupping her hands, she washed her face, stared at bees whirring from bloom to bloom. Despite her resolve, her thoughts returned to Elhamy. She remembered how he had teased her about her shyness. She had fallen in love instantly. His love had been real too. She was certain. Had she not seen it in his eyes? Felt it when his lips first touched hers? Was he pretending? No, no. . . . Had she been born into a family like his, he would have married her. She was sure of this. The more she thought about him, the more she longed to feel his mouth on her face, his lips lightly touching her closed eyelids . . . Only one kiss would have quieted her anguished heart. But Elhamy was gone.

Zaheira's mind was in turmoil. Might Elhamy refuse to wed Mounira after all because he loved her? Maybe he had already declined . . . She had heard his quarreling with his mother . . .

Hope is a ruthless monster. Zaheira's heart skipped a beat. At noon, hearing a car horn in the distance, she ran to her bedroom window to see Elhamy's car arrive. Mounira was sandwiched between him and his sister, just as she had been not so long ago. She heard Gazbiyya's high-pitched giggle, Mounira's deep-throated laugh . . . She would win Elhamy back!

Zaheira washed her face, combed her hair, and put on her prettiest dress and headscarf. She looked at her reflection in her little mirror and whispered, "Gazbiyya will call me down any minute now . . . Elhamy's true feelings will show . . . Mounira is rich, that's true . . . but she won't be as pretty as me . . . anyway, she'll never love him as much as I do . . ."

Hours passed while Zaheira waited. Guests arrived. Voices were raised in recognition of a long-lost friend. Someone shouted a greeting in a language she didn't understand. She heard exclamations of delight and admiration. Laughter was carried up to her by the breeze. . . . From time to time she made out someone saying how much the young people had changed. Zaheira still waited, but Gazbiyya never sent for her. She wept, first out of frustration, then in rage. Finally, giving up hope, she yanked off her pretty dress. To save face she grabbed a passing child and sent word to her grandfather that she was not well and had gone to bed. She bit into her tear-soaked handkerchief, then plunged her head into her pillow to muffle her heart-rending sobs.

Zaheira brooded over every detail of every encounter with Elhamy. She tried to reconstruct the events preceding his last, unforgettable kiss. She remembered their first meeting and every moment in between. Finally, exhausted, she went to sleep and woke up the next morning, resigned. She took to repeating, "I'll soon forget, I'll soon forget . . ." If Elhamy spoke to her she would respond with an impassive face. Poor Zaheira did not know how jealousy's bitter sting would make it impossible to feign indifference!

When Zaheira went to Gazbiyya's room as usual, she found her milk sister radiant and full of gossip. Never suspecting Zaheira's pain, she chattered on about her brother's new fiancé.

"Where were you last night, Zaheira? You should have seen Mounira! She's so pretty, so graceful . . . You can tell from the way she talks and walks and eats that she was raised by the French nuns of Alexandria! She'd put flowers in her hair last night—three right in the front, nestled in a wave. Her hair's almost blond, you know! And her white satin dress was made in Paris! She speaks French better than Arabic and even knows English. She's been to college and plays the piano. She's so lucky . . . She's free to go and come as she pleases. Can you imagine? She's even been to Europe!"

Zaheira swallowed hard. She asked, as casually as she could, "But does Elhamy love Mounira, Gazbiyya? Has she agreed to marry him?"

Before Gazbiyya could answer, Mounira knocked at the door and came in, eager to join the conversation. Gazbiyya greeted her brightly: "How charming you look in that light, flowered dress! How sporty those English shoes are! So smart! I was just telling Zaheira about you. This is Zaheira, you know, my milk sister . . ."

Mounira came in full of exuberance, instantly telling Zaheira how much she loved the countryside, the garden, this big old house, and how happy she was to be reunited with her cousins. She prattled on about her winters in Luxor, her summers in Alexandria, her desire to learn how to drive, to go fast like Elhamy... Every other sentence was in French. Zaheira observed her enviously, hating her. Mounira was beautiful, vivacious, well dressed, rich, and spoiled. She was pretentious and prone to mannerisms, too, and would never make Elhamy happy, Zaheira concluded. How she wished she could warn him!

When Gazbiyya was ready they went downstairs and found Elhamy smoking a cigarette on the steps, waiting for breakfast to be served. He gallantly kissed his cousin's hand, and greeted Zaheira with a quick, impersonal gesture.

"I see you've met out little sprite of Mazghouna, my sister's milk sister, Zaheira," he remarked blithely, turning to Mounira. He was impatient to show her around before the day grew too hot, he declared. He was ready to give her her first driving lesson. Zaheira stood by, embarrassed. Elhamy and Mounira's chitchat, mostly in French, excluded her. Finally, she excused herself, saying she had chores, and ran off.

At noon, she ran into Elhamy alone. His eyes darted right and left. No one was around. He placed a finger on her lips to prompt her to be quiet, then whispered, "Zaheira, "I'll explain later. We musn't be seen together anymore . . ." Quickly, he squeezed her hand and dashed away. He did not see Zaheira's chest heave, nor the tears running down her cheeks.

The days that followed were torture. Zaheira had discovered both love and heartache.

Gazbiyya wanted Zaheira's company even more now that her brother was busy with Mounira. Zaheira was condemned to listen in silence to Gazbiyya's reports about Mounira, her wealth, her dresses, her talents, her wit, her fine breeding, her family... Unaware of the hurt she was causing, she even insisted Zaheira join the cousins on some of their rambles. Zaheira, torn between her wounded pride and her desire to be around Elhamy, went. Gone were the peaceful days before love, spent only in the company of her grandfather! Yet she had no desire to go back to them. They seemed boring by comparison.

Mounira now sat beside Elhamy in the car. Zaheira and Gazbiyya were relegated to the jump seat. Hair flying in the wind, they eyed the couple. They heard Elhamy chatting up Mounira, making jokes, coaching her on the finer points of driving, explaining the engine, pointing out sights, seemingly smitten with his elegant young cousin. Even the old pasha came under Mounira's spell. Amazingly, he did not protest her going out with her face uncovered. Mounira had even talked Gazbiyya into taking off her veil, and her father had finally acquiesced.

Mounira, aglow with self-confidence and the pleasure of her success, gave the orders to start and stop. Elhamy responded promptly to her slightest whim. The conquerer had been subdued.

One day, Zaheira learned from Gazbiyya that the family would soon be returning to Cairo. Strangely, she was relieved. Perhaps she would finally be at peace and forget her dream of a life with Elhamy. Or would she wake from a nightmare?!

A few minutes before leaving, Elhamy found Zaheira alone. Abruptly, he grabbed her by the waist and kissed her on the lips. He whispered, "I'll never forget you, Zaheira. I know we'll see each other again, and I'll explain everything . . . Go in peace."

For a brief moment Zaheira's hopes were raised again. Her heart raced, not knowing whether to be sad or happy. She watched the car leave in a cloud of dust. Elhamy was gone but so was the impossible Mounira. She would not have to watch her eyeing Elhamy, nor listen to her capricious laughter, her interminable French babble. Her precious solitude restored, Zaheira raced from room to room, once again mistress of the empty mansion. She finally ventured into Elhamy's room. The scent of his cologne and tobacco lingered in the air, his bed was mussed, the pillows depressed where Elhamy's head had rested. Like a wounded beast she collapsed upon them, sobbing.

9 ▪ DREAMS

Despite her resolve to forget him, Zaheira was obsessed with Elhamy. She returned to the places where they had been together and daydreamed. She tried to understand what had first drawn him to her and why he had dropped her so brutally in favor of Mounira. Hadn't Turkish pashas of old wed their slaves? Hadn't rich warriors preferred their servants to ladies of the court? Why had Elhamy not picked her? Zaheira's reasoning was subtle. Elhamy, she thought, had tired of his dissolute life in Paris, of the European women that Egyptians were now aping. They pursued men, but then were unfaithful at the first opportunity. Wouldn't he one day regret having given her up? She, Zaheira, would nevertheless love him to her dying day.

Zaheira continued to relive their walks and drives, their playful banter . . . Every detail of their short idyll grew more vivid in her mind. The melancholy songs of love she had grown up hearing had never rung so true!

Sleep brought another dimension to Zaheira's imagination. Although she and Elhamy had never actually gone anywhere without Gazbiyya, in her dreams they walked hand in hand in deserted palm groves and fragrant orchards. They ventured alone into the desert. In her sleep, the chaste Zaheira shivered with pleasure. Waking, she blushed at the visions her mind had summoned. Once, Elhamy had his arm around her waist. He drew her close as they strolled, murmuring words of love. She smiled, promising him eternal devotion.

In another dream, she was reclining on a warm sandhill. Elhamy's lips drank in her eyes, brushed her neck and virginal breasts, kissed her lips. She swooned. Zaheira woke up with a start, ashamed, yet regretful. She would have given herself body and soul to Elhamy had he asked. He hadn't.

One night she dreamed that he was standing beside a young woman, slipping a ring on her finger, smiling into her eyes. Zaheira woke up sobbing. Who was this bride? Mounira? Zaheira? Could the dream possibly be a sign? Would she one day find the happiness she felt she deserved?

Nightly, Elhamy's adored face loomed before her. She saw his dark, laughing eyes. He leaned over her to steal a kiss. In another dream, he stood on the front steps of the mansion in Mazghouna, dressed in a new outfit, telling her he was returning to Paris. He could never marry her. His parents had expressly forbidden it. He could not go against their wishes. He was leaving to try to forget.

The following night, she woke to find her pillow soaked with tears. She had dreamed of a funerary tent being erected beside Roustoum Pasha's mansion in Cairo. Elhamy Bey had been killed in an accident.

Zaheira finally sought out the blind sheikh in the next village to interpret her dreams. The old man did not hesitate. He told her that the young man she described would soon be wed, but he could not see the bride's face. Zaheira knew then that it was Mounira but was unwilling to admit defeat.

A few days later, she wandered in the fields alone and sad. A burning wind blew. The heat of the afternoon made her feel light-headed. She rested on a mound beside the canal, listening to a pump dredging the murky water. She imagined the bowels of the earth itself being churned up. The rhythmic hum became her heartbeat. A field of ripe wheat lay behind her, golden, rustling. Like an invisible hand, the wind set the field to rippling, finally caressing her cheek. Zaheira shivered. She knew these fields, these trees, this canal, yet all that was familiar seemed suddenly strange. She was born and raised in the country, daughter of Fellaheen. She could have lived as the women around her had lived for generations. Why had she been raised alongside Gazbiyya? She had grown accustomed to fine linens and elegant households. She had learned how to pamper her face, delicately paint her eyelashes, trim her nails, perfume her body, dress a certain way . . . She was considered beautiful. Both Gazbiyya and Elhamy had told her so repeatedly. But what use was her beauty if she were forced to marry a Fellah whose days were spent laboriously tilling the soil? Or even worse, a self-satisfied village shopkeeper? Or one of those arrogant overseers who sometimes visited her grandfather and eyed her as if she were cattle for sale?

Once, after Elhamy's departure, Zaheira went into Gazbiyya's room. The armoire door had a big mirror. She cracked open a shutter. In the shadowy room she removed her clothes and fondled her firm breasts, her belly, her thighs. She turned to look at her back, her shoulders, her neck. She wished with all her heart that she could offer her body to Elhamy. How much she longed to respond to his caresses, to feel his burning lips upon every inch of flesh she was touching, to show him the passion contained within her virginal body and soul!

On midday, Zaheira went to the canal. The countryside was bathed in sunlight. Peasants and their animals slumbered here and there beneath a mulberry tree or a eucalyptus. She leaned over the still, dark water and smiled at her own image. She felt a sudden surge of relief and whispered to her reflection: "Elhamy is going to be awarded an important government post! That's what my dreams have been about. He was wearing a new outfit and a new outfit means a new job . . . How could the old sheikh not have know this? Elhamy will be free to do as he pleases. He will forget his parents' fortune and marry me without the slightest hesitation . . ."

She walked home slowly in an illusory state of happiness. Nearing the mansion, a child came running to her, shouting that her grandfather was looking for her. Gazbiyya had telephoned and wanted her to call back immediately. Zaheira ran to the central telephone office in the village, elated. Elhamy was sending for her. She was sure. The operator dialed a number, and Gazbiyya's faraway voice answered:

"Zaheira, my darling, how are you? You can't imagine our turmoil since we left Mazghouna! Where have our peaceful outings gone! We need you . . . You must come to Cairo for the ceremony . . . Elhamy's wedding . . . Don't wait . . . Come tomorrow morning . . . Take the bus to Cairo . . . I'll have a pretty dress ready for you here . . . Just come . . ."

Zaheira was speechless. Finally, Gazbiyya laughed and said before hanging up, "You and I must make every effort to be as beautiful as the happy bride . . ."

The telephone receiver fell from Zaheira's hand. Pale and trembling she went out. When her grandfather asked her if anything was wrong, she blushed, suddenly ashamed of her folly. What was happening to her? Finally she said, "It's nothing, grandfather. I'm just hot from running. Gazbiyya called to invite me to Elhamy Bey's wedding. She wants me in Cairo tomorrow. I told her you needed me here in Mazghouna . . . The celebration will go on with or without me . . ."

"Have you taken leave of your senses, my girl?! How can you even think of refusing?" her grandfather exclaimed. Selim was indignant and puzzled. This wasn't the Zaheira he knew. She would go to Cairo if he had to drag her there himself!

Zaheira did not utter a word in response to Selim's chiding. Looking like a dog unjustly beaten by its master, she hung her head. An image of herself at the bottom of the canal suddenly loomed before her. There, she thought; she would be at peace. She blushed in shame, remembering that she would have given Elhamy her virginity without a moment's regret. Her pride was hurt. She had been overlooked, rejected!

For a long moment she stood, staring fixedly, lips pale, eyes haggard. Then, fully dressed, she lay down on her bed and wept until sleep overtook her.

The next day, she looked for a crack in her grandfather's resolve, but his face was unyielding. It was useless to resist. She would at least see Elhamy again, she thought. He could not miss her imploring eyes and the distress his misconduct had caused!

10 ▪ A MODERN WEDDING

The bus to Cairo was crowded with peasants laden with baskets and surrounded by hordes of kids. Every rut in the road cruelly jolted its passengers. Finally, the three great pyramids loomed ahead, and the bus turned onto a straight, smooth roadway into the city.

Zaheira shook off her torpor, rubbing her tearful eyes. She told herself she must confront what was ahead with courage. She must be just like those great Cairene ladies who turn a blind eye to the betrayals of their men. She sat up straight. The city spread out before her. She couldn't help feeling a twinge of excitement. She mused. Cairo was beautiful, yet you couldn't daydream here for hours on end. Could you even think at all in this noisy metropolis?

Finally, the bus pulled into the station. Zaheira got off and hailed a carriage for hire. The two horses, trotting at a steady clip, conveyed her to the quarter of Helmiyya where the pasha's mansion was located. The streets with their multicolored traffic lights swarmed with people and cars. The crowds were thick and the din more deafening than on her last visit, three years ago. The hustle and bustle took her mind off her pain. She began to realize how Elhamy might not remember their passionate kisses, distracted as one could be by life in the city. Every last minute of Zaheira's country life, by contrast to Elhamy's, was filled with thoughts of the one she loved.

When Zaheira arrived at Roustoum Pasha's, she found only Elhamy's mother at home. The *hanem* kissed her affectionately and instantly began to lament about how times had changed.

"Oh, my daughter, what times we live in! All of our traditions have been turned upside down! Elhamy went off to the barrage with his fiancé and Gazbiyya. Imagine, they even go out alone sometimes! Only yesterday I asked him where he had been all afternoon, and he answered without the slightest embarrassment, 'At Mounira's, then to the movies.' She even comes to fetch him to go dancing at Groppi's. Of course, I don't breathe a word of this to the pasha. He would be furious, even though he's quite taken with the vivacious Mounira. What harm is there in a little modesty? I sometimes think that our young have lost all sense of morality!"

Zaheira asked, "In your day, didn't young women ever go out with the men they were engaged to?"

"Never!" exclaimed the *hanem* without a moment's hesitation. "I saw the pasha for the first time the day of our wedding. My mother used to pin my veil in back so that I would not even be tempted to let him peek at my face. Marriage really meant something then!"

Zaheira ventured, "Do you think Elhamy will really be happy?"

The *hanem* seemed astonished. The question had never occurred to her. Baffled, Zaheira looked away and excused herself. She was determined not to let anyone even suspect she was hurt! She busied herself with one thing and another, waiting for Gazbiyya to return. When she heard her come in later that evening, she rushed to her room. Gazbiyya hugged her and started chattering about dresses, hairdos, the splendid life ahead of Elhamy and Mounira, the operas and parties they would attend, the shopping, the trips . . . Zaheira realized again how foolish her dream had been! What could a simple girl like herself offer beside her complete devotion? What value was her heart to a young man like Elhamy?

At dinner, she finally saw the one who haunted her dreams. His proximity made her uneasy, yet Elhamy welcomed her warmly. He assured her that her presence at the festivities was more precious than the magnificent gifts he and Mounira had received. Gallantly, he kissed her hand and bantered with her briefly. Zaheira saw clearly now that she was nothing to him but a distraction, a game. The tall, carefree young man experienced no remorse at all. After all, if he had dropped his Parisian lovers, why not her?

Zaheira surprised herself. She took part in all the preparations, her pride sustaining her. She spent hours helping to make a party dress for Gazbiyya, visiting all the shops in search of this and that. Zaheira finally found an appropriate outfit, no easy task, given the bold European styles in fashion. She began to feel happier. Gazbiyya coddled her, calling her sister, trying to draw her out. Zaheira knew better, however, than to confide her secret. She would have been the laughingstock of the household. Imagine a servant falling in love with her master, thinking of marriage!

The wedding was set for the following Thursday. One day, Elhamy ran into Zaheira on the stairs, and grabbed her by the arm, saying teasingly, "Are you running away from me, little girl? Have I frightened you?"

Zaheira's heart exploded. She tried to smile, but couldn't. She stiffened. Elhamy, still holding her arm, suddenly realized she was suffering.

"One day you'll understand men, Zaheira. You won't blame me then. Do you think I'll ever forget those days in Mazghouna? You looked fresh as a flower, proud and untamed as a gazelle . . . Won't you still love me just a little, Zaheira?"

Zaheira stifled a sob. Looking away, she whispered, "Ya Sidi, I am your devoted servant. I wish you every happiness."

Elhamy pulled away without another word. Zaheira was determined never to let him see her crying. Her pride had won this battle. Henceforth, she would find solace only in the bitter joy of dignity. At four o'clock on Thursday afternoon, the entire family gathered at Mounira's house to formalize the marriage contract. Elhamy had insisted on a simple ceremony. The contract was signed by the bride's and groom's fathers and witnessed by two uncles. Tea was served for the men and a light buffet for the women. Ignoring the protestations of Elhamy's parents, the couple spent the rest of the evening alone, walking in the gardens of Gezira. Each returned home that night. At dawn the following day, their honeymoon began. They departed by pullman train to Alexandria where they boarded a luxury liner bound for Naples.

Roustoum Pasha's house seemed sad and empty with Elhamy gone. His mother complained about the off-hand ceremony. Taking Zaheira into her confidence, she said, "My child, I think we must be coming to the end of the world. Have you ever seen such a wedding? A tea, a buffet, a hundred or so friends, a few handshakes, and God speed! I've known all along it was unwise to send our son to Paris. He returned with so many strange ideas. We don't understand each other anymore . . ."

Zaheira answered, "Yes, Sitt Hanem. Elhamy Bey has become a Parisian. I don't understand him either . . ."

The *hanem* added, "Every time I proposed a proper wedding, he answered, 'Why bother with these shenanigans mother? What's the point of these useless formalities? The money spent on boring banquets can give us a whole month of honeymooning abroad!'"

"How selfish young people are now!" exclaimed the *hanem*, bemoaning the death of traditions.

"Weddings used to last seven days! Gifts were sent in cartloads all week! The bride and groom and their families would entertain guests all afternoon and evening! The couple would change outfits at least three or four times!!"

Looking sad, Elhamy's mother whispered, "I'm not sure if my son will be happy . . . Mounira will always be running off to Groppi's, to tea dances, to bridge parties . . . What will become of their home life? I have a strong premonition we're going to regret this choice . . ."

11 ▪ SHEIKH GAAFAR'S THIRD WIFE

Roustoum Pasha's big house in Cairo felt empty with Elhamy gone. Gazbiyya was lonely without her brother. Her father was always busy, and her mother was melancholy, perpetually lamenting her son's departure. She was rarely allowed to go out alone. She imagined the young couple onboard ship, watching moonrises above

Mount Vesuvius, dancing in ballrooms of great European hotels. Envying them, she began to wish for marriage herself.

Zaheira returned to Mazghouna as soon as she could, despite Gazbiyya's entreaties to stay and keep her company. At home, in her quiet countryside, she could let her tears flow without being questioned. She would follow the example of the resigned and courageous village women she knew who worked from sunup to sundown. Her ever-loving grandfather would be her comfort now as he had been when she was a little girl. Looking after him would be her solace. She would bury the memory of Elhamy, his words and caresses. One day, she thought, she would be able to smile at her youthful hopes and the foolish dreams of those fleeting moments.

When she returned to the village Zaheira resumed the familiar gestures of everyday life. Resolved not to think of the past, she threw herself into cleaning and organizing. Often she seemed befuddled, however. When her grandfather questioned her, she answered vaguely. On occasion, watching the sunset from the terrace of the big house, Zaheira's eyes searched the desert for something, perhaps an image of a happy couple, laughing and embracing. Would she ever again know that love?

Her grandfather became certain now that some secret was devouring his cherished girl. Zaheira seemed suddenly older. She had grown thin and wan. Her black eyes had lost their luster. Worried, Selim asked advice from some of the older women in the village. After long, noisy discussions they agreed that the change in her was to be expected. Nothing was wrong with Zaheira that a good husband could not fix. Selim reproached himself. He had selfishly held onto his granddaughter, waiting for a signal from her. Now, he decided to take it upon himself to find her a husband. He looked around him for a likely prospect, someone worthy. His friends and fellow villagers lauded the young woman's beauty and virtue and told him that none other than Sheikh Gaafar, the village mayor, would be suitable.

Sheikh Gaafar was a tall, robust man in his forties. His elegant dress and imposing black beard gave him a look of importance. He was regarded as a leader in the community by both peasants and merchants. Astride his ebony steed, he was regal. Everyone greeted him with respect. Women gazed with awe from behind their veils, eyes shining with admiration. He was also feared.

Sheikh Gaafar had two wives and five daughters. Everyone knew he was vexed not to have a son. Marrying again was clearly the answer. Pleased with the idea, he nonetheless approached a third marriage with some trepidation, aware that the presence of a pretty young wife would, without a doubt, cause an upheaval. Since his first wives were unable to give him sons, however, he resolved to act.

Sheikh Gaafar knew Zaheira. She was young and beautiful. She was also better educated than a girl should be. He could do nothing about that. On the other hand, her bond with the pasha's household was to his advantage.

Selim, unhappy to be parted from his granddaughter, nonetheless resigned himself. Better wed her to a man like Sheikh Gaafar than someone less worthy of her. Ceremoniously and delicately, the men negotiated the marriage. Sheikh Gaafar proved generous with dowry and gifts. The wedding was costly and elaborate, the celebrations attended by the entire village. The pasha and even Gazbiyya and her mother came. Lambs were slaughtered and roasted for several days. The villagers gorged and feasted and made music. Children played, and there were games organized particularly for the village boys. Zaheira observed the activities around her with a sad smile, reluctantly admitting to herself that her girlhood was ending.

Although Gazbiyya was full of compliments to the bride, she was embarrassed at the idea of Zaheira being one of several wives. She couldn't help questioning her. Wouldn't she feel jealous? Zaheira shook her head, never confessing that only Elhamy's attentions to Mounira caused her to suffer.

Sheikh Gaafar owned a brand-new house some distance from the village. It was a rich man's house, a new brick structure with large windows and several balconies, surrounded by a garden. Because custom would never allow her to live alone, Zaheira was accompanied by the sheikh's elderly, widowed aunt who would help keep house. The rest of the family—his other two wives and daughters—remained in the village.

Three times a week, Sheikh Gaafar had dinner and spent the night with Zaheira. Sometimes, he dropped in to pay her a visit or have lunch. Zaheira accepted him passively. On her wedding night she had submitted to her husband with neither enthusiasm nor distaste. She even thought of "the other" when Sheikh Gaafar took her in his arms. No kiss would ever again move her as Elhamy's had. She neither wished for nor expected anything. Her days flowed by uneventfully, placidly.

When Sheikh Gaafar married Zaheira, he offered his other wives and their daughters "jealousy gifts." Each had received several new dresses, gold bracelets, and ankle rings. They were mollified, even visiting Zaheira together at first and then separately. They advised the young woman as to the sheikh's tastes, and on the best ways to win a man's heart. Old hands in the intimacies of marriage, they spared Zaheira no details. She listened with vague distaste. She was available to her new master, resigned, but unwilling to make any extra efforts to please him. She observed the rivalry between Sheikh Gaafar's other wives but did not get involved. Sitt Mabrouka gloated over the younger Sitt Satoota's fall from grace, replaced by Zaheira. Sitt Satoota repeated that her rival deserved no more consideration than she did, even as first wife, as she had only borne daughters. Both regarded Zaheira with envy and mistrust yet tried to win her over to their side.

Satoota was thirty-five years old and still beautiful. Her skin was very white, her bosom firm and ample. She went to great lengths to keep Sheikh Gaafar's interest in her alive. When he married Zaheira, she was fearful until she noticed the younger woman's indifference. Her husband would soon lose interest. And if Zaheira were to give the sheikh a son, all the better! His nephews and male cousins, who were waiting like vultures for their share of an inheritance when he died, would be thwarted!

Zaheira's days came and went, dull as the muddy waters of the canal. A year after her marriage, she became pregnant. Gazbiyya visited soon afterward and told her that Mounira was expecting a baby too. Zaheira felt a twinge of the old ache. Why couldn't she have been the one carrying Elhamy's child? Zaheira regretted her own marriage, which had given her neither love nor peace of mind. Her husband was dutiful, but had no interest in her hopes, dreams, sadnesses. He only wanted a son.

Zaheira rarely left home. From time to time, she heard news of Elhamy from Gazbiyya. She was sure she was all but forgotten. Only once had she ventured back into the garden and the mansion, walked across the canal to the desert where she had first experienced love.

Overcome with emotion, she quickly turned back, vowing never to return.

Suddenly disaster struck. A typhoid epidemic ravaged the countryside. Villagers died like flies. Old Selim was one of the first to go. As Zaheira grieved for her grandfather, her husband and his first wife were struck down, followed by one of their daughters. Zaheira shed a few tears and lamented being pregnant. What would become of her child now that its father and protector was gone? She had to close the house that Sheikh Gaafar had given her and move to the village to live with Sitt Satoota.

A few months later, on a cold winter night, Zaheira, aided by her co-wife, gave birth to a baby boy. She named him after the prophet as was the custom for firstborn sons. Pale and tired, she smiled at Mohammad and couldn't help thinking how pleased and proud Sheikh Gaafar would have been. It was too late.

The entire family was in mourning. No celebration welcomed the birth of this child. Zaheira, soon active again, looked after her baby as if in a dream. A strange passivity had enveloped her. She remained indifferent to Satoota's gossip and unceasing chatter. Her entire life became condensed into a few years, a few memories of times shared with Elhamy and Gazbiyya.

Although Zaheira was still beautiful, her face was now marked with suffering. Lines formed around her mouth and dark circles under her eyes. As a widow, however, she no longer had to hide her sadness. She mused freely about the past, unafraid of the tears her memories would elicit. Only eighteen months ago she had existed happily in Gazbiyya and Elhamy's glow...

Rocking her baby at night, Zaheira thought of her crumbling life and lost dreams, and she wept.

12 ▪ SEASHELLS

One spring day, Zaheira sat in the courtyard of her house beside the oven and nursed her baby. The air was warm and sweet, perfumed by mimosas in full bloom. Pigeons cooed and flapped their wings, the males puffing out their chests in a dance of courtship. Zaheira was melancholy and lost in thought. Satoota fussed over her, solicitous since their shared husband had died. She had brought her a wizened fortune-teller, highly recommended by some cousin. The old woman's thick face veil, worn over nose and mouth, was studded with an array of silver coins, indicating her Bedouin origins. A crimson headscarf was tightly wound around her head, hung with amulets. Her black eyes were lustrous and thickly outlined with indigo kohl. She greeted Zaheira with flowery salutations, then squatted, lowering a basket from her head. She fished for a dirty handkerchief knotted on all four corners, untied it, spread it out before her. Carefully, she placed five seashells upon it. These, she explained, represented two men, two women and a child. She instructed Zaheira to bring two of the shells close to her lips and whisper her troubles into them. Zaheira obeyed. The Bedouin scooped up the shells, made a fist and rattled them, murmuring an invocation to the king of the spirit world: "Ya, Kabil, grant me insight. Ya, Kabil, let me see what I need to see . . ." Finally, she threw them down with a flourish and said, "Look, my child, a man that you desire is separated from you by a woman. This woman is your rival." Scooping the shells up again, she repeated, "Ya, Kabil, grant me insight, let me see what I need to see . . ." Once more, she tossed the shells and paused before explaining: "Here is a man standing between two women. He doesn't know which one to pick . . ."

Zaheira's heart raced. Since her husband's death, Elhamy had crept back into her thoughts and dreams. Recently, she woke up certain that Elhamy had not altogether forgotten her. Now, the seashells concurred. She followed their movements with intense emotion. Once again the Bedouin rattled them, her voice rising, "Ya, Kabil, grant me insight! If this woman and this man are to be reunited, let me be the first to witness the mountain between them melt away!" She tossed the shells. The man had turned his back on Zaheira's rival and a tiny shell was behind hers, a child! Her shell self faced up, drinking in the azure sky.

Zaheira, who had never been superstitious, began to find some solace in magic. Also, she was desperate to confide in Gazbiyya, to see Elhamy again. She knew she must not. Trusting the soothsayer's predictions instead, she waited. The very next day, Gazbiyya telephoned from Cairo. Zaheira was to call back immediately. She rushed to the central telephone office on a donkey, her heart beating wildly. Gazbiyya, on the other end of the line, informed her that Mounira was unwell and did not have enough milk to nurse. Her son, Gamil, was growing weaker by the minute. Could she find a wet nurse, someone healthy and clean, and promptly dispatch her to Cairo? Zaheira's heart skipped a beat. Without hesitating, she answered that she and her baby would come. That was, of course, the answer Gazbiyya was hoping for. A car would be sent to fetch her, Gazbiyya told her. Zaheira could hardly wait.

"Your babies will be brought up side by side, just as you and I were, my little Zaheira!" Gazbiyya exclaimed before saying goodbye.

Zaheira tried to collect her thoughts. Had she acted out of a sense of duty? Was she going only because she longed to be near the one of whom the seashells had just spoken? She dared not even whisper Elhamy's name. She put aside her guilt. The life she had been leading was not for her. She was made for something finer . . . She dreamed of being with Gazbiyya, far from the noisy gossip of village women!

Gazbiyya and her mother waited impatiently for Zaheira and led her directly to Mounira's room. The young mother had been crying. Her eyes were red, her cheeks sallow. She was unhappy but sat up and kissed Zaheira, who could not help pitying her, but involuntarily shrank away. She could hardly wait to see the baby. Would he look like his mother? His father? Tears welled up in her eyes when Gamil was placed in her arms. She covered the infant's face with kisses.

Zaheira donned the white silk blouse traditionally reserved for wet nurses and tied a white kerchief around her head. It set off the purity of her features. She was still beautiful.

When Elhamy returned from an inspection tour of family properties in Upper Egypt, he found Zaheira with the baby in her arms. His look of warmth, this thanks, his sincere gratitude filled her with untold joy. She stopped him when he began to rebuke his mother for making Zaheira wear the costume of a wet nurse, a servant.

"Mother! Don't you realize Zaheira's a mayor's widow? That she owns land? A house? That she's your own daughter's milk sister?!"

Zaheira blushed, smiled, and hastened to say, "Your son, Elhamy Bey, is the light of my eyes. I will cherish and care for him as my own and protect him with my life. It is my happiness to serve you in this way, to see my son and yours raised together as Gazbiyya and I were."

Elhamy looked fixedly at Zaheira. His eyes were tired. His face had lost the happy-go-lucky expression she had seen upon his return from Europe. He was no longer the carefree young man who had stolen her heart. She looked warmly back at him. She had never held him accountable for having seduced her. She loved him. In that instant's exchange, she realized that he had not forgotten her.

Zaheira did her job well, lavishing a thousand attentions on the baby. In the middle of the night she rose to nurse him. Sometimes, instead of going back to bed, she sat gazing at the two, little, pink faces asleep side by side. One, born to a rich father, was destined to enjoy all the privileges that life had to offer. The other, fatherless, would be raised in the country, destined to a more-rugged life. Zaheira, however, was treated with every consideration. A household servant was put at her disposal. A special washerwoman was hired to do both babies' laundry. Daily, Zaheira ate her meals with Gazbiyya. As to Mounira, although her illness did not seem serious, she gradually withdrew, more interested in socializing than in her home life. She was always in a hurry, visiting the infant only a few minutes every morning, distractedly asking after him at the end of the day. Mostly, however, she questioned every mirror in the house.

Zaheira's antipathy for Mounira grew. Soon she realized that the young woman was not liked by her mother-in-law, the *hanem*, either. Cold and undemonstrative, she was clearly a disappointment to her husband too. Zaheira began to pity Elhamy. Loving him as she did, nothing in the world made her happier than to serve him, content to be the sweet shadow he would come to depend on. She would make herself indispensable to that demi-god whom she respected and revered.

Elhamy was often away. When at home, however, he sometimes dropped in, took his son up in his arms, spoke to him softly, and kissed him tenderly.

Zaheira expected nothing, wished for nothing other than to live under Elhamy's roof and make him happy. A few weeks after her move to Cairo, when he thanked her profusely, remarking on how well and happy the baby looked, Zaheira was moved to tears, tears of joy!

13 ▪ SERVANT AND CONCUBINE

Time passed. Elhamy's son was weaned. Gamil was learning to talk and babbled gaily to his beloved wet nurse. He went to Zaheira to be comforted when he was teething or had taken a spill. Zaheira dreaded the day when she would no longer be needed and would have to return to the village. However, the pasha's wife begged her to stay. Discreet, warm and efficient, she had indeed become an indispensable member of the family.

Gazbiyya was married the year that Gamil turned two. The festivities were lavish. After the wedding the young woman left her father's mansion for her husband's in Alexandria. She seemed happy. Once she became a mother she rarely visited Cairo but looked forward to her family's spending the summers with her by the sea.

Elhamy's features grew coarser with time. He developed a paunch, became moody and dictatorial. He seemed bitter and was rarely home. When questioned by his wife or mother, he answered vaguely: he had work to do or was calling on friends. His mother suspected an affair, maybe several. She confided in Zaheira as they chatted on quiet afternoons when the children were napping. Perhaps he was having a fling with those Italian women from the opera companies that toured Egypt or with the sensual Hungarians from the music hall. Friends and hangers-on benefited from his largesse and encouraged his dissolute lifestyle.

Mounira also suspected him of infidelity. Pained at first, she began to ignore her husband. Selfish and cold by nature, his absences made her even more so. She spent her afternoons and evenings in elegant drawing rooms, socializing, gossiping, and playing bridge. Like some of her Greek friends, she took to sleeping late. Preoccupied with fashion, she preened for hours before her mirror, talked endlessly on the telephone, interspersing her sentences with "darling," and "dearest." She did not seem to have any lovers, however. Gossip had it that men were not drawn to that hard, steely face. While Mounira never betrayed her husband, she nonetheless took no interest whatsoever in his family or home life. Morning and evening she made perfunctory visits to the nursery, wearing sumptuous, low-cut dressing gowns or tailored suits. She pecked Gamil on the cheek, said a few words to him in French, or scolded him, then left for her social rounds. Zaheira took the toddler out to play, entertaining him with a thousand tales from the country.

The *hanem* confided her disappointment to Zaheira, sometimes weeping with frustration. She often lamented: "In my day, I would have died of shame if the pasha had come home and not found me waiting for him! I was always up before he was. I never entertained these dissolute European ladies who spend their time trading gossip and names of dressmakers and hairdressers! I looked after my children's clothing and linens myself. Zaheira, a husband needs these attentions. Does Mounira even glance at her husband's wardrobe?! Has she ever touched one of his suits or even looked in on his room?! Does she even know if his shirts or handkerchiefs are properly laundered or in need of mending?! Have you ever seen her set foot in the kitchen?! She knows Elhamy likes to eat . . . But putting those manicured hands in flour or folding a handkerchief would demean her excellence!"

Zaheira listened without responding. The *hanem* continued her lengthy harangue, "As for her son, I can't even think how she neglects him! As long as you're here, Zaheira, I won't worry about him. I'm still vigorous enough to run the house and supervise the servants. But when I die, what will become of our family?!"

Zaheira nooded. She squeezed the *hanem*'s hand, assuring her that she was as devoted to Gamil as if he were her own flesh and blood. Elhamy's son and her own were growing up. Soon they would go to school. She would have more time to attend to household matters and supervise the servants. After the *hanem*, it was Zaheira they sought out for direction anyway.

What the *hanem* particularly could not forgive Mounira was her neglect of her husband's clothing. The task was left to a manservant.

Mounira responded cooly that Elhamy was impeccably dressed before he married. Why not now? "Is it my job to crease his trousers and sew buttons on his shirts?! He's spoiled. I'm not his mother and will never be like her and her needlework devotees!" The *hanem* had always ironed and mended the pasha's undergarments herself. She would never have dreamed of letting a servant make her husband's bed unsupervised. She herself had helped him on and off with his jacket morning and evening, and even tied his tie.

"My heart aches when I see what's happening to my son! Elhamy deserves a loving wife!" she declared.

Zaheira averted her eyes. The *hanem* said to her, "One day I couldn't hold my tongue. Mounira was lounging on the sofa and Gazbiyya was here. I said to her, 'Get up and help your brother on with his jacket since no one else will!' Mounira stared at me and burst out laughing. She didn't even budge! The insolence of that woman!"

One December night, the *hanem*, coughing and sneezing, complained that the jams for the year had not yet been made. Date season was nearly over and not a single jar had been put up for the winter.

She began another diatribe against Mounira: "Can't she see that I'm sick! Would she even know how? What did they ever teach her at the fancy French schools she attended? To read novels?"

Mounira treated her like a fossil from another age, Elhamy's mother sobbed. Had she no feelings, no consideration whatsoever? "She might at least offer to help, even if she doesn't mean it! Does she think that servants run a house? If I make the slightest remark to her, Zaheira, she answers insolently. Just the other day I hinted about the jam, and she answered, 'Why go to the trouble when we can buy it?' Well, to my dying breath I'll never allow one jar of Swiss jam or English marmalade into my home! That's a point of honor! Our women have always been proud of their homemade jams, cakes, sweets, and pastries! If Elhamy had taken a firmer hand with his wife none of this would have happened!"

Zaheira listened but did not comment. It was not her place to do so. The next day, however, she rose before dawn, went to the kitchen and carefully weighed sugar and fruit, took down the heavy copper pots, and made the date jam. Elhamy's mother did not hide her pleasure. That evening everyone exclaimed on the delicious confection. The dates were plump and rosy, the syrup delicate. Mounira reluctantly admitted that they were superior to anything one could buy.

Zaheira's delight was in pleasing Elhamy. Henceforth she took it upon herself to prepare candied fruit perfumed with jasmine, mint, or rose water, confections that every self-respecting Egyptian woman takes pride in making at home.

Mornings, she took to bringing Gamil to his father as he breakfasted. One day, Elhamy hinted that he missed the homemade rolls he was used to having with his coffee. Zaheira reported this to the *hanem*, who exploded: "I just don't have the energy to make them anymore! Do you know what Mounira said to me when I asked her to help? 'Such tasks should be left to old women and ugly wives who can't find a way to a man's heart save through his stomach!' Her majesty has more important things to do, but never hesitates to serve our confections to her friends! Well, he's just not going to have them! Elhamy will learn to live with things as they are! Who told him to marry this poor excuse for a woman?!'"

Zaheira remembered the car outings in Mazghouna and how Elhamy's parents had encouraged this marriage. She couldn't help thinking that if the pasha and his wife had deigned to consider her, a humble village girl, they would have made their son a happier man.

The following day and every day thereafter, a platter of the master's favorite rolls—light and golden—appeared on Elhamy's breakfast tray. He suspected Zaheira. One morning, in front of little Gamil, he thanked her, looking deeply into her eyes as he had done in happier days at Mazghouna. Zaheira felt her blood burn.

Going into his room later, she thought again of Mazghouna. How happy and carefree she and Elhamy had been that summer when he returned from Europe! How desperate she had become when he left! Now, living under his roof, she was not quite a servant, certainly not a spouse. Her unquestioning devotion to Elhamy had brought her security, even satisfaction and a modicum of peace. Yet, she loathed what was ultimately a servitude unrewarded by love.

Zaheira shook herself, quickly brushing away such thoughts. What was the use of brooding? She looked around the room and promptly began dusting books and photographs. However, despite her resolve, her emotions got the better of her. She felt Elhamy's presence so intensely in this room it made her dizzy: the rumpled bed, his pajamas on the back of a chair, his dressing gown carelessly left in the bathroom, the masculine scent of his cologne, his body. No other man had had such an effect on her. Like a wound opening in the very core of her being, Zaheira's passion reemerged. She experienced a tightness in her chest. In his mirror, she saw that she was getting older. No one would ever again desire her or want to kiss these lips that Elhamy had so passionately kissed eons ago. A widow, she would never again experience a man's body beside her own. She was alone and would always be alone. The man she would give her life for was barely aware of her. He ran around town, neglecting his wife and forgetting the one who loved him . . . Suddenly, Zaheira found herself weeping.

When Elhamy's manservant entered the room, she regained her composure. While he cleaned the bathroom, she decided to put fresh sheets on Elhamy's bed herself. She organized his closets, sorting through clothing and linens that needed mending. In the afternoon, as the children napped, a hush fell over the house. Zaheira worked contentedly. She sewed missing buttons on Elhamy's shirts, pressed his ties, and darned his socks. The *hanem*, finding her thus occupied, embraced her with utmost tenderness.

"Oh, my child, if only we had had the foresight to pick you instead of that heartless doll! We were blinded by superficial considerations. I should have known better that misbegotten day in Mazghouna! Everyone would have been happier and little Gamil would have had a real mother! You, Zaheira, would never have refused to have more children with the excuse that motherhood spoils a woman's looks or that motherhood deprives us of life's finer pleasures or of precious months of travel!"

One day, unable to contain her rage, Elhamy's mother sternly admonished her son. Had it not been for Zaheira, nothing would get done at home. They owed her what little order and tranquility they had. It was she who ran the house and was raising his son!

"Bless the day she came into our lives! What would I have done without her! Do you think my old legs still carry me up and down these stairs as they used to? She supervises the servants, holds the keys to the stores, pays the tradesmen who deliver, shops, prepares your jams and pastries, attends to your room, mends your clothing! Who do you think keeps Gamil clean and impeccably dressed? Mounira Hanem now even takes her for granted! Lord knows what more she will ask Zaheira to do! Your father has always said that a man who does not impose his will is despised!"

Elhamy, inured to his mother's diatribes, was silent. She continued, "I hope I never live to see the day when Zaheira decides to remarry and leave us! You can tell your Mounira that she doesn't know a good thing staring her in the face!"

Shortly after the *hanem's* outburst, Zaheira did indeed receive an offer of marriage. Sheikh Gaafar's nephew, who had always been smitten, finally got up the courage to ask for her hand. Zaheira pondered. At home, her departure was spoken about with trepidation. Even little Gamil sensed there was something wrong. He clung to his nurse and cried. Zaheira finally asked the *hanem*, who couldn't in good conscience ask her not to marry. Still, Zaheira decided to decline the offer. She had made her place in Roustoum Pasha's home. She could not envision herself living in the village, surrounded by chickens, turkeys, sheep, and gossiping peasant women. When she announced that she was staying, the family could not do enough to express their gratitude.

Elhamy grew more attentive. Zaheira had been a quiet presence, always smiling, always helpful, lavishing affection and attention upon them all. When he came home from some business meeting or from the polluted atmosphere of some casino, he could be sure his son was safe in her care, calm, peacefully asleep, secure in his little bed. Elhamy realized what a void her departure would have left. He became more keenly aware of this young woman he had so easily taken for granted. She was still beautiful. She was still the Zaheira he had played with as a boy, passionately held in his arms in the desert outside of Mazghouna.

Tired of the sophisticated and cold Mounira, of his senseless affairs with other women, Elhamy realized he had never stopped loving Zaheira. Her calm demeanor, the melancholy expression that had etched itself on her face over the last few years, drew him back. Her bright eyes had grown more guarded, her quick laughter had been replaced by a tender smile. Was that resignation he saw in her dark eyes, or love?

Elhamy was pensive, his whole being suddenly suffused with sadness. His dissolute life, his trysts, were empty of meaning. He cherished his son, Gamil, but Mounira, a presence in his home, occasionally in his bed, had become a stranger. He responded to her haughty disdain with cynical betrayals. He would have warmed to tenderness had she made an effort to win back his heart. Elhamy needed to be loved unconditionally. Mounira, passionate in their first months of marriage, had become obstinately indifferent, never even attempting a caring word or doting gesture.

Elhamy's thoughts turned again to Zaheira. He remembered their idyll, the fresh, innocent face that had greeted his return from Europe. He conjured up images of the young Zaheira running through the orchard, disappearing between the trees, returning from the garden, her arms full of flowers. He longed for that inexperienced mouth kissing his, the feel of her closed eyelids touched by his lips, the sound of her sweet voice murmuring with pleasure!

All night a vision of Zaheira haunted Elhamy's waking dreams. He was restless and feverish. He once again burned with longing for her. How could he have been so blind? Could she still be waiting for him? As the light of dawn appeared behind his shuttered windows, he got up, slipped on his dressing gown and slippers, and padded downstairs. He gently rapped on Zaheira's bedroom door. He knew she was always first to wake in the house. She opened promptly and nearly cried out, startled. Elhamy's haggard expression and burning eyes spoke worlds to her. She flushed with embarrassment, still in her nightgown. Her heart raced with emotion. Elhamy stepped in and closed the door behind him.

"Zaheira, Zaheira," he whispered, "You sleep alone in your room and I in mine. I can't stop thinking of you. My life has been a stupid waste. Do you still remember our kisses? . . . I still dream of those few hours of real happiness, Zaheira . . . I know now that I have never stopped loving you . . . And you, Zaheira? Do you still have a little corner in your heart for Elhamy?"

Zaheira blushed. Elhamy took her gently by the shoulders, looking intently into her eyes. She gestured with her hand toward the room where the children slept. He squeezed her hand and went to close the adjoining door. She couldn't move. Elhamy turned, gently kissed her eyelids, his lips trembling. She responded, quivering. He took her into his arms, embraced and caressed her. She sighed. They fell together upon the still-warm bed she had only just left. At last, they were united in love, discovering the passion for which they had both so dearly longed.

When Zaheira regained her composure, her heart was filled with joy, and her face was radiant. She snuggled against Elhamy's shoulder, inhaling the scent of the man who had for so many years haunted her dreams.

Finally, she murmured softly: "Yes, I do love you Elhamy. I've always loved you. I'm your birthright, and I knew you would come to me one day. I'm only a humble servant, but I'm yours forever."

Rising, she tucked the sheets around Elhamy, who lay languid and calm, head resting on his arm, a smile of deep satisfaction warming his face.

Zaheira washed and dressed before him. He was her husband by right, her soulmate. Now, she felt no embarrassment whatever around him. Before her mirror, she raised her arms above her head, combing her hair. Elhamy was struck by the beauty of her neck, her shoulders, her full breasts.

Gazing at Zaheira, he suddenly remembered a tune. He sang softly as he had not done for years, years of loneliness, years of deprivation:

> Every man longs for paradise.
> Every man longs for heaven.
> And I, and I,
> I've found my heaven in your love.
> You appear and
> my home is filled with magic,
> these old stones suddenly aglow.
> The garden murmurs in your wake,
> the rustling of leaves at my window, more enchanting than
>   the sweetest song.
> The trees sway to the rhythm of your breathing,
> and the sound of water from the thousand streams of
>   paradise gladden my heart.
> Your face, beloved, is my shelter,
> your love paradise, your love
> the closest thing to heaven . . .

Thus began a new chapter in the lives of Elhamy and Zaheira.